# There's a Ma
# and (



James De Llis

~

Cover design by Djordje Matic

*Dedicated to the county of Norfolk, UK*

# Contents


| | |
|---|---|
| There's a Man Crying in the Street | 6 |
| The Armoured Man | 24 |
| The Lane | 42 |
| Wet Sock | 52 |
| They Looked Like Old Tall Dolls | 60 |
| Sleeping Thomas | 68 |
| The Checkout Woman is Dead | 74 |
| The Cruise | 82 |
| A gentle light all made of blue | 116 |
| Thoughts and Memories of Violet | 138 |
| The Shed | 156 |
| Bone Feet Don't Have Hair | 166 |
| The Place That's Green, Like Seafoam | 198 |
| Yeah, it's okay, I'll wait in the car | 218 |
| Some People Livin Just Ain't Made for Life | 222 |
| The Townplace | 228 |
| After All Things, Maybe | 240 |

# There's a Man Crying in the Street

Mum?

Yes dear?

There's a man crying in the street.

What?

The girl stood by the lounge window looking out into the front garden, holding the curtain over one side of her face, peeping out into the world. Past the greasy fingerprint smudges on the windowpane, across the small lawn, on the other side of a generic square hedge there stood a fully grown man. He had his hands brought up to his face, cradling it. His shoulders were slumped, head slightly bowed, and he was all held together with a damp rotten, sullenness. It was an overcast day as the day before had been. The week had been generally dreary and the month much the same, everyone here waited for some day lost in time.

There's a man out in the street and I think he's crying.

What? said the mother again with a sense of urgency, as if this was a sort of threat and yet also, moreso, something she most certainly didn't want to deal with.

Look! Just come here! He's right here out the front and he's crying.

Okay I'm coming one second, she said all at once as she stopped preparing dinner and strode through to the lounge. She stepped close next to her daughter and squatted as to see what she was looking at. See! He's right there! And he was. He was there. In front of the house all stood and half-bent over, all limp.

Yes, I see him.

I think he's crying, the daughter said. The mother didn't reply but only kept looking forward toward the man. I said I think he's crying mum.

...well...yes, he might be, I don't know. Come on, come help me with dinner.

But what about the man?

I'm sure he'll move on, now come on, the mother said as she stepped back toward the kitchen.

Okay, said the girl letting out a sigh. Before she stepped away, she leant closer to the window and accidentally bumped her forehead lightly against the glass. The bump resounded and it trembled the mum's gut and the daughter said Oops and looked up to see if the man had heard the bump. He had not moved from where he stood, but he had turned toward the window. Mum he's looking at the house kinda, the girl said.

Get away from there right now and come help me with dinner! the mum half-shouted in a single breath as she stepped back into the lounge to grab the daughter. Okay okay, I'm coming. But the mum got there before the girl had started to move and hastily grabbed her arm, and yet she couldn't help but look outside once more and the girl was right, the man was looking. He was looking at nothing and into nothing and through the window and through his fingers and through them and through everything. His fingers were all wet with tears and half dirty and his face was all pulled contorted like a baby's loose-skinned weeping and there was trembling and the mother caught what should have been eye contact. Two-thirds of an eyeball making connection and she was shown the pathetic innards of that man out there crying in the street. It made her feel sick and annoyed and grumpy and scared, but mostly sick, nauseous and all acidly gooey. She pulled sharply on the daughter's arm, pulling her away. She checked the front door was locked and strode into the kitchen.

Forget about it for now. Come on, let's make dinner, the mum said with all the uncertainty everyone attempts to keep at bay. And it was all coming down now and no one was secure and there wasn't any threat but tummies trembled and lower lips tried and the quiet could not be filled with thought nor sound. Nothing had really happened and yet everything had been invaded.

~

The father arrived home just as the dinner was being served and placed quietly onto the table. There's a man outside in the street, he's-

Crying?

Yes. It seems so.

I saw him too daddy.

Huh, I'm sure he'll go away.

Yes, come on, let's eat.

Chippies!

The father looked at the mother and the daughter ate her chips.

Eat the veg too dear, or no dessert.

Yum chippies yes okay, the daughter said all quick and happy.

The father hastily ate his dinner as the mother slowly ate hers, the daughter oblivious to what was apparent on the other side of life, the matured world. Cutlery clinks and little sounds of digestion filled that piece of the neutral that no one could ever own and no one wished to leave alone too long. The father finished up and tapped the table a few times as he shot a look to the mother. Just gonna check something, he said. And up the father was and into the lounge pretending to check the sofas, behind the cushions, and tapping more tabletops, flicking a slow glance at the window and then, with bravery he thought silly, through it. On the other side of the hedge was the figure he had glanced on his way inside, still there, half covered and appearing to hide himself, half behind a tall hedge to the left now. All shrunk and not there but there. The father closed the curtains.

~

In the morning all was erased from memory and yet reality stood firm. The father waking early, a few minutes before his alarm, a body clock tuned to expectancy. The mother slept quietly all curled up and holding onto any sheet available, hands clasped.

He went downstairs and prepared his flask of tea and his flask of coffee and his lunch for the day. The early morning tremble of being permeating all things, the death of twilight clutching at the last as the father rubbed his face, packed his things, and set foot out of the front door to work. Brisk and cool, cool and brisk, with a touch of dizziness and repetitive fatigue. Eyes heavy and drooped stepping through a light frost on the lawn towards his van. A little crunch here and there, quiet quiet. Holding the handle of the van door and pull and click and sit and pull and click. A gruff cough that brought forth cold phlegm. Another rub of face and forehead, hands on the wheel, eyes front. The thinning frost but circling the windshield. There he was.

On the pavement some 30 feet ahead. All sullen still, droopy man, a little figure of overflowing despair in god's dead world. Not to be missed when in sight and yet forever hidden. An ontological stench. There he was. Curled over, hands to face. The father tilted his head to the side as many do, as if to get a better look. The crying man turned a little more toward the father's van and took a subtle step. The father sat up straight and started the van. The crying man took another step. The father turned on his lights. The crying man slowly brought his hands a little from his face. Skin pulled in and down and up and all over like some melting foetus grown ancient. Tears streaming and then pooling in the pockets of pulled flesh. The trembling and the snivelling and a single audible low moan that held in the air like a calf crying for its mother in the morning mist.

The father pulled away slowly, passing the man on his left. The crying man returned his hands to his face and bent forward some more. As the father reached the junction at the bottom of the hill, he held steady and checked his rear-view mirror. The crying man was walking away, up the road and into town.

~

At lunch the father took his place among the usual group of weathered men lost to the muck of it all. One of them had a tattoo of a dashed line around his neck with the words 'CUT HERE' front and centre. One of them more shoved his lunch down his throat than ate it. One only smoked, and another too. One grunted and another agreed and another held his smoke a little longer in his lungs on sporadic puffs. Lots of dirt on the hands and they were all cracked and the dirt mixed with the bread of repetitive cheese sandwiches.

Go on tell us one then Billy.

Ah, not today man. Knackered.

Ah, go on.

Fuck off.

Ah fuck off yourself. What you eatin?

Cheese sandwich.

Yeah.

A ripping belch with bits of splutter and grub and decade old dank tobacco.

Fuck's up with you?

Nothin.

Fuck it is.

Nothin, get out of it.

Eh, whatever.

And they all sat and finished their lunches. Occasionally cigarette smoke would waft too thickly into an eyeball and cause it to water and sting. Nothing more was said for there is a casual respite in deep misery. One of the men watched Billy pack up his stuff and slowly walk off to go back inside. Half-hastily he pushed off the wall and caught up with him.

I say, what's goin on man?

Just tired man.

Nah, nah, you ain't.

Well, I am, but it ain't that.

You seen him?

Huh?

You seen him.

After work chap, we gotta get back.

Sure.

They headed in and fired up the machines again. All quickly forgotten, the blare of extraction fans once again overtook everything. They all placed their ear muffs on and lunch wasn't even a memory now. Spitting chips of wood and dust and the air was dry in an instant. But as quickly as it had all started up and hands became once more worn it equally all fell down the other side of the day and ended. Same old aches and coughs, odd quiet haunt, the fact of mandatory continuation.

Aye, everyone else is gone, he said as he waited leaning against a rail outside, puffing deep on a cigarette.

Alright, let me get the door.

Billy locked the door and checked it again and again not wanting to face him. Eventually he turned, he had to, as to go anywhere at all.

Yeah, I seen him. What of it?

The man?

Which man, plenty of men arou-

The man crying. He was crying.

Yeah. I seen him.

And he was crying?

Yeah.

Crying?

He was crying.

Yeah, he was.

So?

Ain't right Billy, something there ain't right.

Aye.
Billy began to walk away, looking back at his fellow colleague.

Ain't right Billy.

See you tomorrow, Ken.

Yeah, he said as he sauntered half-scared off to his van.

Billy got into his own van, sat back, rubbed his face and hair with his dry hands, held the key in the ignition and looked forward into the certainty of the dirty windshield. Nothing held. He drew a deep breath and shook out a chill, preparing for the short drive home. Pulling away with a brief glance back to his fellow worker's van.

There he sat, hands holding the wheel, body still, face sunken to somewhere he never wanted to go, not today, not ever, please. An emotion reserved for some other time beckons its head in the now and you just weren't prepared. Billy looked back to the road as he clicked the radio on. In an instant the vacuous shite faded from sensory reality and he had only his thoughts and the static of driving to accompany him. You can only escape so much.

Billy found himself within town without knowledge of movement or direction, the traffic all bundled nearer the centre like busy ants. Waiting behind a dirty old truck, looking aimlessly at the shops surrounding him, catching a reflection within a shop window of a woman striding and leaning and clutching, all forward. As the reflection disappeared the reality came to pass and he saw the woman in true form pelting down the road, what appeared to be her dizzy husband not far behind her, looking back and then forward, checking for something, as his pace quickened. The traffic not moving.

The man in the truck in front leant out of his window and looked back down the road and his brow went puppy-eyed as a child ready for a foul, foul beating. He quickly snapped himself back inside the cab. Nothing was moving. Billy looked in his sideview mirror and saw a group of people in the street behind him. Checking the rearview mirror the group was ten or so thick. Huddled close and tight and tense. Nothing was moving still. Billy decided against all pleasant and regular impulse and got out of his van, with legs not of his own, as always in such cases.

Closing the door without looking Billy began slowly pacing toward the small crowd, to see what's goin on, as the old folk would say if they were here, but they're not, they're all gone now. And there was a chill and a small wind and they added nothing and were ignored by all. Billy became one with the crowd and their camaraderie was instant. Battle and defence may bring men together, blood even more so, but nothing glues man to fellow man like fear, and there is no fear quite as potent as plain old grotesque discomfort. No one wants to take responsibility for the non-violent horror lest they get infected. And though Billy pretended to wonder what they all were looking at. He of course already knew and so he stood with them looking at the man he'd already seen.

He was in the centre of the road crying still. The group stood together, shoulder to shoulder, looking upon him with they as one and he as nothing. The road held flat into a dead junction where cars passed as fleeting stripes of colour. The shopfronts on either side made of paper and barely holding to anything at all, for it was that no eye could see anything but the man that was there, and he was crying. Dead centre.

The crowd got snug and he was more and more dishevelled as if his being was becoming splayed over the tarmac. A little ragged coat was a little ripped. A woman amidst the group had bad indigestion and kept hard swallowing. Another felt a tad dizzy. The crying man still bowed over in front of them, crooked back and chin to chest, nothing tight, everything only sunk and if he could we all imagine he would simply sink into the primordial gulf like a spool of sputum wretched out from life.

Sir? a man in the crowd said as if someone else had said it and a woman sighed and another managed to file off and Billy kept his eyes on the man. He stood with his right side to the crowd, the profile shining black as a stinky crow whose feathers had all withered down and down. His response to the beckoning was one of a slow turn, the head rising upwards from the chest and attempting a heavy arch toward the crowd, shoulders following, and finally the two tiny tap tap steps needed to bring him round. A woman in the crowd going weak at the knees but held upright by the pressure of the mass. And the man was still crying, just weeping, right there, a man near coated in tears, pouring they were, running in trickles. He finished his abattoir pirouette and faced the crowd. A few more peeled away, appearing as flashes of clothing gone in an instant, the woman's knees finally gave and she collapsed onto her chin which split open at the flesh. Billy held his tummy and let out a hollow, prolonged Oh. The mass shrunken to a frozen few who had but no choice. There he was and there he was and they wished quietly that he wasn't. His eyes came up first, to meet theirs. The lids had swelled and caved in from all sides, a sadness compounded from his moment of expulsion trying to cover all chance of sight. His hands were no longer on his face, he had allowed it to open to the world, however crooked it and he might be. So now his fingers fiddled with themselves in eternal nervousness. Tears visibly pooling in the corners of his eyes, mouth pulled down at the sides, tremble tremble all over. Oh, little child what did you not receive?

His mouth starting to stretch open and he trying to hold it back, teeth rising, nose scrunching, sniff and sniff, and a deep groan almost from behind him, like the pain was there before and he happened to find himself in its place. As if to but open his mouth at all would release pain upon pain and a misery none of us wish to admit to. But he did and had to and was in the middle of the road. This poor contortion of flesh holding the apple's full weight. Nothing else was there, nothing that mattered. Billy wanted to step forward but didn't. Billy wanted to cry but didn't. Or maybe he couldn't. The man crying in the street pulled his face back to his chest and walked on down the road. The remaining few watched him until he was out of sight. A few empty seconds passed and the members of the mass looked at one another and none accepted nor admitted to what was and so they all went back to the normality that is.

~

A week passed. Billy found himself avoiding the town center but a notice had come through his letter box about an upcoming town council meeting. Once before he had sat on the board. For a year, like most, until he realized it was merely a way for dying old people to feel like they have power in a world that knows they're dying. The notice said simply it was 'A Meeting for

Those Concerned.' Billy told his wife and she said he should go and so he went. Though there wasn't a date on the notice. He knew it would be that night at 7pm. It'll be in that old building, his wife said.

Yeah.

What you think about that building?

The council one?
Where they'll have the meeting, yeah?
Same as so many of them, no thoughts really.

I think it's all mothy and old. It shouldn't be there. Lots of buildings shouldn't be here. Don't you think?

I don't know.

All those foisty carpets, no insulation, always too much space and everything echoes.

I ever tell you about the old toilets outside that building?

The town council building, no?

The ones that had the long ramp and cold iron rail for wheelchairs?

I know them.

I remember a long time ago, maybe my earliest memory, because I was young enough that the bar was near head height.

Yeah?

I was stood waiting for someone; I don't know who. And I was just waiting, and I remember looking at the bar and someone had carefully draped a raw pork chop over it.

Draped?

I remember it looked like it had been carefully placed on the bar. Not thrown or anything.

Oh, a...?
A pork chop. Raw. There was no packaging around and there was just this single, pretty thick, raw pork chop draped over the bar.

Draped?

Yeah, it was delicate. It's a delicate memory.

How could that happen?

You know, I can't even devise a theory, never have.

Me neither.

One of those things.

Yeah.

Are you coming to come with me tonight?

No, I don't think so. No. I'll stay with Janey.

I understand.

~

The evening arrived. Billy parked up in town and made his way up past the building. He hadn't eaten much recently and felt nauseous, too nauseous to eat. But that's half of life, he thought, having to do something you don't want to do just so everything doesn't get worse. He walked up to the entrance with his head down and shoulders high, it was cold out, but he didn't really feel much now. The door was open so he drifted in without transition and found himself sitting amidst a large crowd. Every seat was filled in fact. The noise of their chatter held a constant pitch and when Billy held to a thought it was like he was more alone than he'd ever been. There was a comfort in that misery he couldn't admit to. Nothing warmer than misery, he thought. He held his hands together and they felt so dry.

Okay! half-yelled the man from the town council. Okay, let's start this meeting. But there was a long pause. People looked at one another and all knew but no one wanted to know and no one wanted to begin. I guess that's how it might be tonight, he said.

We all know why we're here, said a man in the back, non-existent.

Yes, I suppose we do.

So, what are you going to do? said a panicked woman at the front.

Well, we don't really know, because...

Because what?

Well, what is it? What is this?

We don't want him here! yelled a young woman holding her baby.

There came a unanimous agreement from the crowd in tones of muffled yeses and ayes and hear-hears and indeeds and that's rights and mhmms and everything all at once in a quick spirt and then it fell and it was quiet and horrible.

Any objections?

Do we know who he is? said an elderly man at the front.

Okay, well, we will work something over the next couple of days. said the town council man. We'll get it done, thanks to you all for coming.

Billy heard it all and recognized it but didn't take it in or process it. He sat until most everyone had left and spent that time looking at how flaky and old his skin had got.

That's time for ya.

Huh? Billy replied.

I see what ya lookin at, I been there.

Billy looked up and saw his old schoolteacher.

Blimey, long time Mr...Smith?

We all have to die Billy and I can't teach you outta that corner, he said angrily as he was walking away.

Billy shrugged it off and finally got up and headed to the exit. He passed the town council man talking to two dead-eyed gents. There were many yeses and okays and rights and then Billy was out of earshot. The outside air crept up on his skin but he quickly glazed back into nothing and found himself back at home before he knew it. How did it go?

Yeah, they're going to sort it.

Good.

Yeah.

Yeah.

They looked at each other and accepted something and then something else left and wasn't coming back and it hurt because it was quite vital and vulnerable but you couldn't know that until then. But that's always the way, too late can only ever be too late, otherwise we'd be different people.

~

Little Janey, little Janey! Sprinting into town, gigglin and laughin and skippin and hoppin. A smile pushing her cheeks to maximum velocity and dimples descending into a grin of greatness. Clutching at a little bag of pic-a-mix she'd just bought. Little froggies and snakes and milk bottles and cola cubes and fizzy bottles! Running and clutching and opening and quick to grab a little sweet and throw it in her mouth and chew and chew and laugh! So aware and awake she caught every reflection and every light and everyone seemed to know her and many would say Hi! and Hello! and Hey Janey! and she would jump and shout back and many might laugh. Running and running further into town to meet some friends and have some laughs and there he was still weeping and taking everything. She stopped her stride and felt quite sick, she put the sweets into her pocket and didn't want to go on but she didn't really stop walking toward him. Some 30 feet away, though she had felt sad, she began to smile lightly once more and continued walking forward with the bag of sweets in her hand and then a van pulled in front of her and parked on the curb and looking through the back window to look through the front, she saw some movement of cloth and heard a slam and they pulled away slowly and he was gone. She waited a bit and then took her sweets from her pocket and began to eat them again. Slower, now, and she tasted the crunchy sugar before the flavour now. After a few she'd had enough. Such as it is with these things.

# The Armoured Man

There are two-up two-down houses that mirror one another on a street that is repeated 40 times over in each and every direction. Sometimes the neighbours looked out of their windows at each other's porches, driveways, and back gardens, sometimes at the spaces in between all things. There the trees were exactly upright and there the leaves lagged behind a dead wind and every object held firm to gravity as if it were no longer theory but the only fact. Children and teachers walked home from the local school that was just around the corner from everyone's individual house. On the walks home no one spoke and the only pairs were from families. Some of the families had one child, some had two, and some had more. There were a few dogs that stood in the driveways with all four paws clamped to the floor and with eyes that looked forward into nothing at all. They would bark when people walked into their line of sight and the bark would be immediate, a shrill instant tear that lingered only in memory.

It is dinnertime and outside a drawn-out shriek ran through life and then died out leaving a silence that destroys marriages. Inside the two-up two-down sat a family of three. A mum, a dad, and a young daughter. They are seated around a circular table. There is a big bowl of colourless salad in the middle and they each have a single porkchop plated before them.

How was school?

Good, thank you. How was work?

Good, thank you. How about you, dear, how was work?

Same old really, busy.

That's life hey! replied the mum and no one laughed.

Dad?

Yes dear.

When I was walking home from school and passed your car on the street...

Yes...

Well, I think someone has scratched it.

He didn't say anything and stopped cutting the porkchop exactly where he was, leaving his knife diagonally shooting up from the plate, the fork almost adjacent. He walked out of the front door and the mother and daughter looked at each other. The mother seemed sad and the daughter felt guilty but she didn't know why.

The father re-entered the house and sat down again. You're right, someone has scratched my car. Then he grabbed his knife and fork and simply stopped. His hands began to tighten around the knife and fork. They squeezed them so tightly the knuckles appeared as if they might burst through his skin. His fingertips were pooled with blood, and all hot and red. He stared straight forward through the kitchen wall, through everything.

Nothing to worry about, hey dear. He let out but a small, barely audible grunt from his closed mouth. Come on now, let's finish our dinner said the mum.

The mum and the daughter slowly ate and looked anywhere but at him. He hadn't moved. His hands clasped to the cutlery, fingers digging into his palm, nails penetrating the flesh. His breathing had become that of a dying engine, a hiss through the teeth, followed by an almost panicked intake as oxygen became fully depleted. Gasping at air now only as a quantity.

The mum and daughter finished their dinners. The mum placed a little more salad from the bowl onto the father's plate. Well, we'll leave you to it. Come on dear. With that the mother and daughter got up and went where they always went. The mother went and sat in the lounge and looked at the TV and thought about all the time that had passed her by and about how it might be cathartic to just fucking die right there and then however painful. The daughter went upstairs to her room and did her homework. She'd been told to write the number 71 as many times as she could on a piece of paper. Last week was 70. She said to her mum last week that she was noticing a pattern and could fit it many times onto the paper. Her mum said that was good then so she assumed it would be good now too. She began writing the numbers as a barely audible soap opera tune dampened the air.

Sometime after she had finished writing the numbers and then spent some time staring into the wall and then the pillow the daughter figured she would need a glass of water. She went downstairs and into the kitchen. The father was still there, grasping wretched through matter itself. With eyes wide and bulging and getting teary, yet still bloodshot and tired. The daughter passed before him. His only movement was that caused by her gentle breeze, not even his eye refocused as his hands continued their sinew destroying grasping.

She stood in front of the sink, turned toward the father, sipping her glass of water. He was still, internally stretched, tensing further and further. She was about to say something when the mother appeared from behind her. I think it's about time you went to bed young lady.

Okay mum.

She looked at her father and pushed a smirk.

Come on, off to bed.

With that the daughter walked off with her glass of water and headed back upstairs. The mother sat opposite the father and looked directly at him. Her eyes locking with his. His eyes glazing over and through her into all the non-space that ever was.

You know, it *is* just a scratch dear.

She could hear his teeth grinding down upon themselves, his jaw creaking at its delicate joint. The lower eyelids trembling a little. Lips pressed into thin red lines. Face tort.

Well, I am off to bed dear. Turn the light out when you come up. But he didn't come up.

The morning arrived and the mother and the daughter went downstairs for breakfast. Would you like sugar on your cereal?

Yes please!

Okay, but I won't put on loads, we don't want you bouncing off the walls.

The mother carefully put down the bowl of cereal in front of the daughter and grabbed herself a banana and a pot of yoghurt. They both ate quietly, looking here and there in the room, occasionally glancing at one another. At the table remained the father. He had not moved. Blood was welling to points of tension such that his skin had become an odd mottled patchwork of red and white clumps. There was gunk in the corners of his mouth and he breathed through his nose in spurts. Much on today at school love?

I haven't checked my timetable, but I think I have art.

Oh, exciting!

Well, I'll wash up and you get your stuff ready for school.

Okay.

The daughter got up from the table and ran upstairs to her room. The mother dumped the bowl in the sink and binned her banana peel and yoghurt pot. She turned and looked down at the father. Looking closely at how all his neck muscles were strained and rippling, as if a sheet of paper could slice them into segments. His eyes were pooling with water at the bottom. She stood behind him and tried to pull his head back. It wouldn't budge. More forcefully she attempted to arch it back so the tears would wet the eyes, but nothing moved. From directly behind him she placed both hands over his forehead and leant back with all her weight, his neck and head suspending her from falling. She leant as far back as she could yet he did not move. A small, almost indiscernible squeak escaped from somewhere in him. The mother stopped, grabbed a glass of water and poured it slowly down the front of his head, all down his face. It dripped off him and he didn't move and the table was wet and she could hear only dripping.

Get a grip. she said under her breath.

The daughter ran back downstairs. Ready.

Your lunch is on the counter, see you later on dear.

Thanks mum. Bye.

And with that she left for school.

~

The mother sat herself across the table from the father. Once again staring at him as he stared through her. I will call the doctor she said with slight scorn. As she pushed off the chair to stand up, she heard a light snap, a little crack. Then turned her neck to swiftly look at him to find that his chin was now pushing into his chest, with his eyes still looking upwards toward their previous point of focus.

I will do it right now, she said.

The mother stood in the conservatory, adjacent to the kitchen where the father sat. She took the phone off its holder and twiddled its wire with her finger as was her habit. A little time passed. Time she spent looking through the doorway to the kitchen at the father in profile. Brows down, chin to chest, jaw tight, neck taut, shoulders high, belly firm, arms straight, fists clenched, back curled, feet planted, and toes pressed. He was a circuit of tension whose purpose was to cancel out difference. All that rippled over him were further waves of strain and apprehension, visible ripples of a further descent long since agreed upon.

Hello...yes, this is Mrs M...I am calling about my husband...the problem is...

The mother moving before him from the doorway, phone cord pulled and wrapped tight around her finger, leaning down as to hold her face before his. His eyes deep into the pit of that which he couldn't accept. A little infant in there with tears of joy eroding, a small child in there with limbs exploding, a teenager in there dying, the adult out here in the now it has given itself over to. Lips indiscernibly pulling down and up, up and down, trembling into themselves as to hold it all back. Snivelling, snivelling. The father's entire head stroking itself into a vibration that pulled the air into him. The mother wide-eyed, whites surrounding the iris as she retaliated against this embarrassment of etiquette.

Hmmph! He is all tense and tight and strained and I don't know what to do...I tried pulling but he would not move...this afternoon?...3pm...okay then...thank you.

The mother straightened up, unwrapped the cord, and placed the phone back on its holder.

The doctor is going to be here later, maybe you heard! Anyway, you'd best be better by then. I'll be in the lounge if you need me.

She walked away.

For goodness' sake. she said under her breath.

And the mother sat in the lounge alone watching another soap opera and the father sat in the kitchen alone entirely pulled, falling into himself as a ligament rips against its own attempt at grasping.

~

At 3pm on the dot there was a single, sharp bang on the front door. The mother promptly pushed herself off the sofa and quickstepped to the door.

Hello.

Hello. the doctor said.

He is in the kitchen, just here.

Yes. I can see him from here. May I come in?

Yes, you may come in.

The doctor stepped into the house and drew a deep breath in through his nose, arching his head back a little as he did so. Stepping through to the kitchen he quickly stood before the father. He gestured at the table with his hand. Do you mind if I move this?

Not at all. Let me help you.

The doctor and the mother grabbed one side of the kitchen table each and lifted it a few feet away from the father. There he sat, curled over like some dying mantis revering rigor mortis. Arms out entirely straight as the rest of his body curled into itself, his hand still clutching at the fork which now bent a little from the heat and tension.

Has he moved at all since he got like this?

The father let out a sharp breath from his nose.

No.

Oh. Well, let us try move him to the floor for now. Perhaps best to clear this room.

Okay then.

The doctor and mother set about emptying the kitchen of all furniture except the chair upon which the father sat. They moved around him and he held fixed firm. Outside a bird flew by in a sweep. None of them witnessed this. Once the room was void of anything but the three, the chair, and the tension, the doctor walked behind the father.

What I'll do is try lift him from under his arms and as I do can you push the chair out from the side?

Yes, I can do that.

The doctor did as he said he would and gripped under the armpits of the father, finding he had to push his fingers forcefully between arm and torso. The mother came to his side, half-squatted, and gripped the underside of the chair. She looked up at the father, shook her head slightly and rolled her eyes at him.

Okay, when I say to, try get the chair out and I will then lower him to the ground.

Okay, I can do that.

The doctor looked down his nose at her, took a breath in, tensed his arms, and leant back. Okay, go.

Okay.

The father moved as a single unit, there was nothing that could be called a joint or curve. He was being held but an inch above the chair. The mother trying to pull the chair from under him. Now hastily trying to yank it from him. His legs adhering, weight toppling down, feet planted to all they knew. Fully squatting now, grasping at the chair, pushing off the floor whilst leaning far back. The doctor felt a small bead of sweat run down his right armpit. The mother's feet slipping from under her as she accidentally pulled herself halfway under the chair. The doctor promptly dropping the father back onto the chair.

Let's take a break here for a bit. We shall try again in a minute. he said as he placed his hand on the back of the father's neck.

The father sprang with a piercing crack into the shape of a plank. His head driving up under the doctor's chin, splitting one of his molars into mini pieces that rolled around in the bottom of his mouth immediately, the doctor being forced back against the wall, losing his footing and tumbling to his knees. The plank father being dragged by mandatory gravity forward to the wall, cheekbone first he slid down the paintwork, stopping waist-height from the floor. He leant now as a human rafter.

The doctor quickly got to his knees and ran to the sink, his mouth automatically opening and allowing a slurry of bone to fall from it. The mother on her back lying next to the overturned chair quickly sprung up and checked on the doctor.

They stood together at the sink as he took sips from the running tap and spat his bloody saliva into the sink. Between sips the mother would say Oh I am ever so sorry about this. to which the doctor would reply It's fine. Just give me one minute. They repeated this a few times before the doctor eventually stood upright. The mother handed him a towel and he dried himself off. Right, where were we? he said, turning back toward the father.

Looking down upon the father once again the doctor saw that he, the father, was entirely rigid. The tops of his feet pushed into the floor and his cheekbone flattened against the wall. Held at something like 45 degrees.

Hmmph, said the doctor.

Stepping forward proudly the doctor raised his right leg and pushed the father over with the bottom of his foot. The father's face sliding against the wall until he eventually hit the floor.

Right. We are going to drag him through to the lounge and place him on his back. Grab his feet.

Okay, I can do that.

Together they carried him through to the lounge and placed him before the fire on his back. Both the doctor and the mother now out of breath and sweaty. The father was cool to the touch, a tad clammy. The doctor once again took a deep breath in through his nose.

He will be fine there for now. I will come by again in a few days to check on him. I think it may be fine, nothing at all.

Okay.

And with that the doctor left.

~

The daughter arrived home from school and went through to the kitchen.

Mother, why is everything not where it normally is?

The mother was vigorously cleaning the sink.

Oh, it's nothing dear. Head upstairs to your room and I'll call you when dinner is ready.

Okay.

When she was finished in the kitchen the mother walked through to the lounge to look at the father. Looking down at him there laid taut in front of the fireplace. Head arched back, toes curling back, fingers spread, skin stretching, with a grimace concealing a tyrannical disorder that sought to understand itself solely from what it already had. The mother walked back through to the kitchen to start dinner. Some time passed.

Dear! Dinner is ready!

Okay mother, coming!

Your dinner is on the side dear. I'm going to eat mine in the lounge because my show is on, you can join me if you like?

Okay.

The mother and the daughter grabbed their dinners and went through to the lounge, one following the other. The mother sat on one sofa and the daughter on another. The mother clicked the TV on and it buzzed to the channel they always watched. A vague soap opera theme tune filled the lounge and the dim light of the TV lit their pale pork chops. The father lay in front of the fireplace, in front of them, off to the left a little, staring upwards through matter. They ate without talking and watched the show to the end.

That was nice, thank you mother.

Thank you.

The father's feet then snapped themselves upwards, so the tops of his feet faced his shins. He let out an almost silent growl between his teeth. Little bits of spit flew out onto his lips and chest.

I will help you with the washing up.

That's fine dear, you go do your homework.

Okay.

The next night was the same, except the father snapped his chin deeper into his chest, eyes bulging and looking down his body.

The next evening his arms cracked toward themselves so his elbows were brought together in his chest. Then he brought his knees to his chest. Then his heels pushed deeply into his buttocks. His hands folding down onto the forearms.

One evening the mother and daughter sat watching TV whilst eating a dinner as usual. They finished the meal and both stood up to take their plates back to the kitchen. The daughter halted and looked down at the father. The mother halted too, looking at the daughter, and then down at the father.

His body was almost a ball of cracked and stretched and torn and taut limbs. Head and face deeply buried into a concoction of cracks and snaps. His breath descending to short wheezes and splutters. Slowly it all began to move toward the other side of its own being, a tension attacking itself. A prolonged squeak reminiscent of a woodlouse dying protruded from the lump of fluxing painful limbs on the floor. The squeak transformed into a deafening onset of nauseating tinnitus. The daughter dropped

her plate and covered her ears. The mother watched as some tomato sauce got on the carpet and rolled her eyes. The deafening squeak was seasoned with snaps and cracks and crunches and stretches and splits and fractures and splinters, all drumming into an unapparent point of armoured cacophony. The father tensed a final time and folded entirely into himself, into a point and then into nothingness. A trembling whimper resonated and held as the final memory.

The daughter looked at where the father had been. The mother looked at the daughter and then at where the father had been.

I've got homework to do.

Okay. I need to get this stain out of the floor now.

~

(Dedicated to Dan Lowe)

# The Lane

A little town. Closer to a village really. The kind of place where people who are forgotten live. There might have been a person of note who once lived there, maybe 200 years ago, but not anymore. Maybe a few people in the town still know that person's name, but mostly everything just keeps on going in a routine of nothing that leads one to death. There are houses and shops, a couple of schools, and a few nameless parks which are just patches of grass with an assortment of decaying metal structures on them. Public things rarely get repaired and most people keep their houses basic in appearance. Nothing flashy, nothing too old, and nothing too new. Most go straight home after work and simply eat their dinners and watch TV. At night you can see the glow of many screens shining with a light amber hue from many windows. Some of the windows still have net curtains. The sky here doesn't change, sort of blue, yet always overcast. The name of the town doesn't matter and no one ever thinks about it, people just live there.

In the houses are families and these families are mostly two adults—a mum and a dad—and then two children. These parents get home from work at different times, often the mum first and then the dad, meaning the mum starts making dinner. The children arrive home from school and sit on the sofa watching cartoons or go up to their rooms and do some homework or anything that is really nothing. In one of these houses, itself five houses in, along a row of identical terraced houses, is a family of just this sort, about to sit down to dinner. They are going to be having spaghetti bolognese, which is one of the roughly eight dishes you might see on the tables in this town.

Kids, dinner! yells the mum.

Okay, says the young girl from the sofa.

Give me a minute, says the young boy from upstairs.

Have we grated any cheese? says the dad.

They hadn't grated any cheese so the dad got up and went to the fridge and got the block of cheese and grated some into a bowl. He looked into nothing at all as he did so. The mum was plating up the dinner and the occasional little ding could be heard when the metal serving spoon hit the ceramic plates. The dad and the girl sat at the table, simply waiting for the food. They had little to nothing to say to each other but tried most days anyway.

How was work?

Oh, same old, you know how it is. You getting on ok at school, good day?

Yeah. We had biology today and I don't really like that.

Oh yeah, ha ha, states the dad staring through the bowl of grated cheese.

The mother finished plating up the food and brought it to the table just as the young boy entered the room, quickly sitting himself down.

Was just finishing something up.

Okay.

For some time there is the sound of clinking cutlery, mastication, indigestion, scratching, chairs moving, a few coughs, and the occasional Mmm. The dad then leans back in his chair, pats his belly to signal something and asks So, what are you kids up to this afternoon?

I'm just going to do some homework, says the young girl.

I'm thinking of popping up the road with Harry, says the young boy.

Oh yeah, where you off to? says the dad, idly looking through to the room where the TV is, his sentence trailing off anyway.

Just a few houses up, the grass bit. You know, The Patch, as we call it.

Oh yeah, I know it. Well, don't go too far, the dad says, casting a slow glance at the mum. Locking eyes they acknowledge something neither of them want to utter and both hope simply will not be and yet both know that if it is to be then there is little to be done. Such is how things are.

Do you need help with the washing up mum? says the young girl.

No, that's ok sweetie, you go do your homework.

Both taking that as being given the okay to leave, the young boy and young girl head off to their respective futures. The young boy quickly running upstairs, grabbing a football, and then just as quickly running back down and out the front door. The dad leaning back on his chair and looking as the door clicked shut and then glancing upwards once more to the mum who was staring dead and heavy into the sink.

~

The young boy jogged up the road holding the ball under his arm. He could see his friend Harry from where he was, seated at the singular bench on The Patch. Hopping a little shin-high wooden rail he landed in the grass and breathlessly greeted his friend, Hey man.

Hey, how's it going?

Yeah, pretty good mate, you? What'd you have for dinner?

Yeah, I'm alright, we had spaghetti bolognese, how about you?

Yeah, same. Fancy a kick about?

Sure!

And with that, they began kicking the ball around The Patch. Passing, volleying, playing keepy-uppy, headers, the full works of football tricks. Harry accidentally booted the ball too hard and it bounced off a nearby low-hanging branch just past the young boy's head and rebounded out of The Patch and further down the road.

Ah sorry man!

No worries, I'll grab it, says the young boy.

The young boy ran out of The Patch and some ways down the road to where the football had stopped. Caught in a dip in the road that was all covered in damp leaves and an indiscernible black sludge. The young boy picked up the ball and turned back towards The Patch. Harry was gone. But this didn't seem to matter. He could even just about see his front door from here. Yet, he felt drawn to look over his right shoulder. He didn't know why. It was like a false wind had whispered a silent command. He looked around, and to the right, and before him was merely another lane of houses, of which he could see the end. A dead-end street. But it just wasn't right. Something up there wasn't meant to be. He did feel a pull, but he also felt very sick. There was a deep ache in his lower stomach and he felt really sad. The sight of the Lane made him very upset. He was cold to the bone and his legs were now hollow. Heading in any direction felt terrible, but he decided to walk home. His front door felt as if miles away and to march there was a feat of deep remorse. Halfway he dropped the ball due to fatigue. It bounced away. He got to the door, looked back, and clutched his stomach a little. As he entered the dad said You're back soon? Where's your ball?

I dunno, says the boy, Gonna head up to bed.

Okay son.

~

In his bed that night the young boy could not settle and yet did not toss and turn. No thought took root and the bed itself was not a physical anchor. Have you ever witnessed the palpable nothingness of what was before? It seeps in. He lays flat. The young boy desired a cold sweat or a headache or to vomit, anything to bring him back from where he was being taken. Of where he could not say and no one can and no one dare. He rubbed his feet back and forth on the sheets to try to develop a place of warmth but he was not allowed. All was weightless and the boundaries were without friction. He sat himself up on the edge of the bed and gazed at the window. His bedroom was situated at the front of the house, and if one was so obliged, they could lean a little from the window and see down the street. He pulled the curtain and the net curtain over his head and shoulders. From behind him all one would see was the bottoms of his legs on tiptoes. From the street, one would see the dark outline of a pale face caught in the gaunt capture of absence. A sullen child gazing into a nothing he sought to know. He could just about see the Lane he stood before earlier. He stared for some time as the breeze passed through him and caused his eyes to well up with tears. A young boy's head protruding from a suburban window, weeping at the sight of something only he can see. His jaw let out a sigh not of his control, a quiet, exasperated guttural sigh from nowhere, out into the world with its dead brethren.

The young boy stepped down from the window in the early hours of the morning. Eyes tired, lips blue, trembling core, and empty empty. He laid back on the bed and waited for anything to give him direction. His gaze overflowed itself and apathetically penetrated everything, his vision could not latch onto material. Sound dulled to muffles with a slight taste of plastic and iron. He wished he could vomit, that would have been an odd delight. He heard the dad's van drive off for work. It must be 6AM. That meant little to the young boy. He laid still, facing upward, with only a single shuffle, for the next two hours.

There was a bang on the young boy's door. Come on! Up you get, you don't want to waste your weekend in bed, the mum says.

Now getting up, says the young boy.

He sat on the edge of the bed and stared forward for a while. It didn't matter. He stood up and proceeded to walk downstairs. Muffled door and overly quiet steps. He couldn't keep his head up. He got down the stairs and went through and sat on the sofa. The young girl was there. Morning, she says.

Morning, he says.

She was watching the TV and the young boy stared at it with her. So, what are you kids up to today? says the mum who leaned in the lounge doorway. I'm going down the park with Jenny soon.

Think I'll just stay in. says the young boy.

Huh, ok. Well, I'll be next door helping with their decorating if you need anything. Don't go too far. She looked at the back of the young boy's head and knew something that she didn't know she knew.

~

Soon all had gone their separate ways and the boy remained sat on the sofa staring at the TV which was just going and going. He got up and went to the front door and opened it. Leaning out and looking rightward he saw the Lane a little clearer than last night. It was there. He was here. He closed the door again, went back upstairs and got dressed. Thick socks, thick jumper, and a small scarf. No material seemed to touch him. He pressed the scratchy scarf to the skin of his neck and it just wasn't. He sighed and felt as if he was going to cry, but he didn't. The feeling that one gets before crying, that vulnerable empty lump in your throat that swells and trembles, that remains and boasts sovereignty. His throat and belly ached and he was cold.

He went back downstairs, turned the TV off and proceeded out of the front door. No one was in the street. He looked both ways multiple times and waited out the front for a good while. No one came, no one passed, and no one knew. He walked slowly up the road towards the patch, thinking back to yesterday to where he and Harry had been. He continued walking and without looking up knew himself to be before the Lane. He crossed the road away from the Lane and leaned against the house wall which was adjacent. The windows of the house were boarded up and the brick was dry and cracked when he leaned back against it. The young boy looked up and into the Lane, trying to notice it, trying to sense it. Complete evasion. Nothing was. He couldn't really get his breath and knew he might not make it home. I guess it had to be. Pushing off from the wall he crossed the road again and headed up the Lane. A young boy clad thick with cloth heads up an unnoticed lane. There are things there that aren't meant to be and yet they still are and there's nothing to be done.

~

Come and get it! says the mum.

Now coming! says the young girl who was in her room.

Smells good, says the dad.

It's Bolognese, says the mum.

She dished up the food and set it out on the table. The young girl had entered and sat down and they sat there and waited.

The front door closed with a quiet click. It was very late. He came through and took his place at the table. The dinner was now stone cold. There you are, says the dad.

Good day? says the young girl.

Eat your dinner, says the mum staring at her, refusing to look over. The dad's eyes cast downward.

The young boy was there but he wasn't. Something else picked up his fork and ate for him and they all knew it but none of them understood it. The young boy looked forward and all around vacantly, unable to be in any direction or in any sense. The dad made a swift glance upwards from his bowed head to the young boy. Looking back, behind the young boy's eyes lay a twitching, laughing absence that was without mercy for anything and all. The dad hastily finished his meal and went to go through to the lounge and watch TV. A little weep. The mum and young girl ignored it. The dad sighed.

# Wet Sock

He would have been in school when it first happened, somewhere in the big field, away from everyone else at lunch. Far away, trying to get them out of sight, so he could eat in peace he told himself, but in reality, he didn't eat anything until dinner. Early food made him feel sick, most food made him feel like that, like he wasn't meant to eat at all. It just sat there, in his belly, his tummy, all heavy and not right.

The grass hadn't been cut and it was damp and raining, drizzling. Two boys came over and one knelt behind him and the other pushed him over the other and he tumbled and he was all wet through down one side. All his back and a little of his side feeling like wet socks and shirts you want nothing more than to rip off. The boys had run off and he found himself sitting in the grass even though it was wet, the coolness was oddly pleasant. He didn't care, and he never would again. It was gone, and that was that.

Eventually he stood up, eyes heavy and full of tears and light rain. He walked to the end of the field, to the fence that looked down onto the road. He placed his hands against it, leant, and watched the cars pass by for the rest of his free time, knowing that the bell would soon ring again. The cars were mostly blue and silver. Soon enough they blurred into one another and he was looking through them, as with all things, once again. One passed by at high-speed blaring out rock music, the sound cracked into his head and lingered as a loop he couldn't forget, as he didn't know its end. It rose and fell over and over; the rest of his free time had been taken from him by some passing noise. Silence is all that matters, he thought. The bell rang.

He sighed and turned, letting his hands drag down the rough steel fence. As he started to walk back to his class his left sock squelched. He wanted it gone. He stopped and pulled off his shoe and, balancing on one leg, pulled off his sock. He stared at the bottom of his foot and found that in pulling off his sock he had pulled off some skin. Where the skin once was there was nothing at all, just a hole into nothingness. A hole in his foot that looked into both nothing and infinity, an impossibility. He quite liked it. It was his, after all. He had spent too long gazing into the abyss in the bottom of his foot and forgot that he was balancing, and so, before he knew it, he found himself slowly toppling over into the grass, glaring into the void as he did so.

He sat there and forgot all about class and all about the wet grass and simply held his bare foot on top of his knee as to get a better look. He tried to move his foot this way and that to get a better look, but from all the angles he could muster the hole looked onto and into nothing. A nothing made of both the space existent if the foot were not there, and, yet also, the space behind that. The structure behind what we might call something. He felt as if in a trance, a wondrously neutral moment that was just for him and him alone. Oh my god! You freak! said a girl from his class passing by who caught him gazing into his foot, late to class.

He shook himself back to reality and looked around, knowing that he had to get to class. But he wanted to sit with the abyss for a while. It seemed friendly, even. Slowly he inserted his finger into the void in his foot. First one finger, then two, then three. The extra third finger pushed against the hole and widened it. It didn't hurt. It felt as nothing at all. He thought he should be scared, but he wasn't, he could finally disappear, he thought. He decided he would put his sock back on and get back to class. Before he did, he ripped a tuft of grass out of the field and threw it into the hole, it fell in-between all space and disappeared. He laughed again, bundled up his wet sock and threw that into the hole in his foot also. Like the grass, it fell into oblivion and was never seen again. Fearing that if he put his shoe on now it might fall into his foot void, he opted to walk back to class barefoot.

~

He walked into the classroom late. Where have you been? the teacher asked him.

I had to go to the loo.

You should have gone at lunchtime.

I didn't need to go then.

Don't talk back.

He didn't go to the loo because I saw him looking at his foot on the field! said the girl who passed him by earlier. The class laughed. The teacher instinctively looked down at his feet and realized he wasn't wearing a shoe or sock on one of them. Come on, the teacher said, put your shoe and sock on, you're not in pre-school! He said he lost his sock in the hole in his foot. Get up here right now young man! He got up front and the class saw he was all wet and covered in grass stains and laughed at him again. What did you say?

Sorry?

You lost your sock...where?

In the hole in my foot.

What does that mean?

This, he said, as he proceeded to awkwardly lift his leg in an attempt to show the teacher the void in the bottom of his foot. She caught a glimpse of it and simply stared forward. See? he said. But the teacher just kept staring straight ahead. He placed his foot back down on the floor. Can I go back to my seat now? he asked.

Go on, show us then! someone yelled from the back of the classroom. Everyone else yelled in agreement. Okay, he said, let me get my chair. He walked back to his seat, grabbed the chair and dragged it to the front, placing it right against the front wall so he could fully extend his leg. He sat down, rolled up his trouser leg, and used his arms to help lift his leg high so the entire class could see the zero abyss in his foot.

A chap to the left passed out, slamming his forehead squarely onto his desk. Two others at the back fell off their seats. Multiple people on the left-hand side had instantaneous panic attacks and couldn't catch their breath. One girl, far at the back, screamed until she too passed out. Some others went into a strange trance alike the teacher. One girl nearer the front vomited in a rather pathetic manner, all of it just dribbling down her front and spilling onto the desk. The class was mostly shaking. All these trembles and worries there now. One of the boys, trying to control himself and regain composure, half-yelled That is fucking disgust-, but he couldn't finish his sentence before he broke down sobbing.

He had never felt more alone and no one could speak. The teacher had sat down and placed her head in her hands, crying, alike the rest. I'm sorry, he said, I quite like it.

Oh god! was bellowed from the back, how could you!

I guess I just do, I'm sorry.

He looked around, and no one was looking at him or the foot anymore, they were looking into their own nothings, trying to get away, as he had always done. He drew his foot onto his knee once again and looked into the hole. It had got a little bit bigger due to the walking. He reached down and slid his entire arm into it, pulling it out again with a smile. Isn't it great?

No! No! again, from the back of the class.

Just...just go, said the teacher, looking out from behind her hands.

Go?

Exasperated and weeping with everything gone. Yes, just go...

Okay, he said, as he sat up straight on the chair, reached down his leg and ripped at the hole, opening it all the way to his knee.

No! Not like that! I meant-

Oh, I thought you meant into the hole?

No, why would I mean-

He continued ripping the hole wider, his entire leg had become pure void as he continued to rip it wide across his groin and down the other leg. Laughing warmly and feeling loved, no one else made a sound. He ripped it open from the groin upwards across his belly and chest, his clothing falling into the hole itself and leaving him sitting as pure anomaly. He crossed his arms and pulled each with the other into hole, leaving his head and shoulders decapitated yet standing in free space, atop an uncanny rupture in all things.

His smile was broad and his eyes creaked with a genuine joy. This'll be great! he said, as he slammed his head forward and down into where his chest would have been, dragging the rest and all of him into the hole. He'd disappeared and the liminality of the hole soon faded back into reality and all was right yet wasn't.

# They Looked Like Old Tall Dolls

Mum said I should never say about them but I can't help it really because I remember the first time I saw them and didn't really know what to do. And, you know, when I said about them before to mum and dad when we were in the car mum just yelled at me and dad was really quiet. But I thought I would tell you about them because I don't have anyone else to tell. The first time I saw them was the time when mum yelled that I just told you about. We were in the car and I was in the back and we waiting at a junction in the middle of town and there's lots of traffic there now because they moved where the buses stop. We were like two cars back from the junction and the road was blocked with buses behind us like I said and so when the cars turned in from the junction they were getting all jammed next to us as we waited to move forward. Dad was annoyed because we weren't moving and he is always annoyed about market days and parking spaces or something, I don't really know, but then he went really quiet and mum was just staring completely forward and I didn't see them then because I couldn't see who was pulling in from the junction. But then a car pulled up next to us, stuck in traffic like us but in the other direction, and then when I looked out of my window I could see into their car. And I remember thinking that it was a funny family all wearing big masks that looked like big round wooden balls on their heads. But it wasn't and mum said not to stare and dad was quiet. But I did stare over at the car and it was a family of four all with these shiny, like...varnished heads, maybe they were bigger than basketballs, like those small globes that you spin, just like that, and all shiny. But I stared because these weren't masks and I know that now and I think I knew it then and maybe mum and dad knew it and maybe that was why I stared, because they weren't masks, they were their faces and they looked back at me all with the same face and look and I think I just smiled and maybe waved. They had, you know, ears and eyes and mouths and all that, and those things did sort of make sense on their heads but the whole thing wasn't right and I think dad made a comment about wanting to just get going or something. The cars in front of us did eventually move forward but I hadn't stopped staring at them and it was clear it was a mum and a dad and then two children in the back. A family of them there was, and they all had this same weird wooden, shiny head, and then when we pulled away they all looked forward again and I saw that their heads turned very stiffly, like maybe they couldn't even look up and down, I dunno. When we finally got going dad drove very quickly and mum bit her nails and looked back at me, but I was fine, and she was not, and dad was quiet. We drove for a bit and it was quiet because the radio was broken or something and then I asked mum what I wanted to ask and maybe what other people wanted to ask but as soon as I tried to speak she told me to just be quiet and not mention it, and when I asked her what I wasn't meant to talk about it she just said that I knew what she was on about. So I wasn't allowed to talk about them and I guess that was just the way it was, but then that was the first time I saw them. I can't remember exactly the next time really, maybe it was a month later cus we never really went out much anyway. But we went to town and were walking through the center, actually kinda near where we had been with the car cus it's a small town, and we were meant to be going to the bank on the corner I think...yeah, we were, cus that was where they were, the people with the weird heads. We were just across the road waiting to cross and they came around the corner and they sort of really looked like a family, all together, all four of them just sort of walking. But it was strange then and I think we just stopped where we were and mum tried to distract me and dad just looked off in some other direction but I have to admit I stared again because now I could see them all. I remember looking at their heads now I could see them better and they were how I thought they would be, you know, round and shiny and looked as if they were made of wood. But then all of them, like, their bodies, they were all the same height but you still knew that two of them were the children and who was the mum and who was the dad. They looked like tall old dolls. I don't know how I knew this but I knew it and I knew everyone else did too. But their bodies were tall and thin, almost as tall as a door, maybe taller, and spindly with these thin arms and legs that looked like they spun on pegs or something. They walked along stiffly and all looked around with those stiff heads and no necks. They were all wearing these patchy sort of suits that didn't fit well and were very baggy. I remember looking around the town and there were a few other people there and none of them seemed to notice them, I think some of them were clearly looking away or even went inside. I remember asking mum who they were and she said she didn't know and that I shouldn't ask and that I shouldn't ask again because it's not something to worry about. But I do remember this very clearly. The doll family kept walking along the pavement in their stiff, thin way, and dad wanted to go and had already walked a bit in the other direction and mum had seen him go and grabbed me by the arm but I was still staring. And I was looking at them and mum was trying to pull me away and as the doll family walked up the path the mum turned her head and looked right at me and they all stopped. They all stopped and the doll mum was looking right at me and the two doll children looked at each other and seemed to speak and the doll dad followed the mum's sight and looked at me too. I noticed them and they noticed me. I held up my hand in a little wave and my mum tried to slam it down but missed. Then my mum looked over at them and saw they were looking at me, and, just before she dragged me away, the doll mum smiled at me with a brown painted smile that grew from nowhere, but I was turned away before I could see anymore. Then there was the last time I saw the doll family, because afterwards things got weird and I don't know what happened. We didn't go to town much anyway so I don't know if the doll family were around much, but I think it was more just that they were around that made some people feel odd. Anyway, we had gone to the other side of town to what mum calls the fancy supermarket to pick up some things to eat over Christmas. We were at the far end of the store, past the fruit and veg, in front of this cheese counter. It has one of those big display cases with a glass front so you can look in and ask for which cheese or ham you want. Mum was talking to the lady behind the counter who I think she knew from when she was in school ages ago, I was looking at the cheeses. I remember trying to see how much the price was on this really fancy cheese but my eye's kept focusing on the light that was reflecting off the glass, and then I remember the light got blocked off by a circle and I was looking at the reflection of the doll mum's head and realized she must be behind us. I didn't think anything of it though because honestly her smile had stuck with me and so I turned around and I remember looking up at her in her weird suit. This patchy suit made of all this thick fabric that hanged down baggy and I could see from here that her head seemed to be made of a thick wood all covered in like a gloss. And I said hello and she didn't hear me so I stepped closer and said hello again and she turned her whole body towards me and bent like from the waist to look down at me as I looked up at her. Her eyes were little painted points and thin eyebrows, her nostrils were points too, her smile was brown paint with white teeth trying to come through, and these little weird ears stuck on the side of her head. Hello little boy, how are you? she said with lips that seemed delayed, as if something else spoke from inside her head and the paint had to keep up. I remember looking up at her and her cream skin was so shiny I could just about see myself in it where the light hit. I didn't really know what to say so I just said I was fine thanks and we just looked at each other and I remember looking into her eyes and feeling weirdly safe and then she smiled some more and her eyes seemed to bulge with some joy found from somewhere else. I smiled back and noticed her awkwardly move her arm from her pocket and swing it forward towards me. A painted doll's hand with all the fingers connected held out some bonbons for me to take and as I went to grab them my mum screamed at me to Get away from him! and ran over, barged past the doll mum and yanked my arm to take me away. As I was being dragged I remember looking back and seeing that mum had knocked the doll mum over and she was just flat on her back in the supermarket staring straight into the ceiling. Just as we got to the front door of the store I pulled my arm from mum's and looked back again. The doll mum had turned her head to look at me and she was still smiling. She seemed sad and angry, but not at me, she smiled at me and it felt honest and I think she was very kind. I remember waving back and then mum took me away. I think after this things got odd or something as they often do when people don't just say about things right in front of them. Because I remember a few nights at home from just after this where I heard mum and dad arguing downstairs and it would be really loud but then it would go quiet and I'd put my ear to the floor and hear dad say things like ...do about them. or What even are they? and no one wanted to mention anything. When we went into town everything was tense and not nice and I didn't see the doll family again. Everyone in town became weird and suspicious and we all looked at each other and we all knew, but then no one knew anything and no one wanted to admit that. There were nights when mum and dad would yell at each other again and dad would sleep downstairs and everything felt hot like it was overcooked and no one said anything about anything. Then there was the night about a week before Christmas where mum and dad fought and he stayed downstairs again but then later on she went downstairs and I crept to the top of the landing to listen to them. I couldn't hear it all but they were talking about the doll family and dad said something about finding them or calling someone or something. Mum said he should just do it and go. I remember peaking my head round to look down from the stairs and mum was stood with her arms crossed staring at dad as he left in the middle of the night. The door closed and I quickly went back to my room. I couldn't sleep. A few hours later I heard the front door open and close so I decided to get back out of bed and peak downstairs again. Mum and dad sat through in the kitchen so I could hear them a little bit better. They were talking about where dad had gone. He'd gone with a few friends or something to find them he said, and they had found them, and they were awake, just sat around their dinner table waiting for nothing. I didn't quite catch it all but I think he said he grabbed one of them and took them out of town with his friends. Said he didn't really know what they were going to do or something like that but things got out of hand and they were angry. I remember this, though, I remember specifically that he said the head cracked open into pieces and there was nothing inside. After I heard that I felt sick and went back to bed and cried. A few days later we went into town for the Christmas lights and the town was absolutely packed with people. There were carols and food stalls and live bands and all that kind of stuff. But I remember that this year the announcer with the microphone wasn't as lively and no one seemed to enjoy their food and everyone was looking at one another and everyone knew something wasn't right but no one said anything. We didn't stay long, no one did. When we got home I went straight to bed and thought about the doll mum and her children and when I got in bed I cried because no one knew anything and she'd offered me sweets and her smile was nice. A few months later we moved away and mum and dad pretend that it never happened and that no one in that town felt weird or odd about it all. But often when I look at mum she knows what I'm thinking about and dad goes quiet like he used to.

# Sleeping Thomas

Getting up to much tonight, Thomas? he imagined them asking him.

Mostly sleeping, he imagined himself replying with the utmost sincerity. And yet, as always, the man in his imagination as all men in his imagination had always done half-laughed in reply. Ha! Isn't that the truth!

Others had replied: That's how it is for sure—Such is life—If only— Cor, what I'd give for that—Gotta 'ave dinner first though—C'est la vie—Chin up pal—Weekend soon—Soon be Summer—Soon be Christmas—Not long until a holiday I imagine—Early one, 'ey? —Yeah, I know how you feel.

But they didn't know how he felt. He had analysed all of their feelings on a spreadsheet some years back and concluded that actually none of them knew how he felt. It was fine that they felt as they felt, but they did not feel as he felt. He had equally concluded that if it were that someone else felt exactly as another, then surely each of their respective steps from then on would be mirrored. Maybe, he thought. But also, he knew they didn't feel how he felt because his statement, the one about sleeping, was a truth. One of the few he knew for sure, in fact.

He would, indeed, be mostly sleeping. He had imagined the words 'mostly sleeping' over 1300 times this year alone and not once was the imagined reply a lie. Split into the two parts 'mostly' and 'sleeping', Thomas truly was going to spend most of his night sleeping—as always—but only most because he needed sustenance. He would arrive home, drink a nutritional shake, and then get into bed and fall into a programmed sleep.

He had done so ever since he had become terminally bored with life. So much so that he found sleep, in its purest form, far more interesting. Dreams annoyed him. When I am asleep, he thought, I want to be asleep, I do not want this half-life nonsense. When Thomas awoke from a dream, he felt duped out of time within his own personal abyss which was, by all rights, his to take. I want to do that which means I am not, he often thought to himself. The closest he could achieve to this ideal was to sleep as much as possible.

He was 24 when he started what he titled 'Notes for Non-Engagement'. It started as a quick draft on a single sheet of paper, the aim of which was to maximize as much sleep as possible on any given day. That is, a calculated means to not be, as much as it was possible to not be whilst one still is. Sleep is the answer. Yet, what started as one sheet of paper is now 17 full notebooks. Thomas soon found that each and every moment of one's life could be maximized to allow for more sleep. And so, as it is, and would always be, Thomas spent his time from 24 onwards sculpting his life so he could exist in the greatest possible state of non-existence.

Thomas worked as a car park attendant. A private structure just across from some corporation's headquarters. Thomas didn't know who employed him, he hadn't asked. He attended the car park in a daze. Thomas worked the night shift, 7pm to 7am. The corporation closed down at 5pm for the majority of workers. Thomas was there for no reason he could ever discern. In fact, an addendum to volume two of his Notes lists every single interaction he has engaged in whilst working in the car park. A total of 8:

01/04/1981: Man told me where the induction VHS was, asked if I needed help playing it, and told me to put it back once I was done. I told him I could do it and okay.

13/04/2001: Man walked in and asked if I knew any taxi services. I said I didn't.

16/09/2003: Man came in and informed me that a mechanic would come tomorrow and work on the barriers. I said okay.

17/09/2003: Mechanic working on automatic barrier asked me where the toilet was. I told him where the toilet was.

18/09/2003: Mechanic working on automatic barrier asked me where the toilet was. I told him where the toilet was.

19/09/2003: Mechanic working on automatic barrier asked me where the toilet was. I told him where the toilet was.

20/09/2003: Mechanic working on automatic barrier asked me where the toilet was and how long I had worked here. I told him where the toilet was and that I had worked here 22 years.

01/01/2011: Man came in and thanked me for my service. Gave me a box of chocolates. Told him I didn't eat them. He left them anyway. I threw them in the bin.

He sat in a small office with a window that looked out onto the two barriers that let cars both in and out of the car park. In theory, drivers could press a button that allowed them to speak to Thomas if there was ever a problem. In theory, Thomas was fully prepared and trained to deal with all manner of basic and complex problems. In practice, there was never a problem. After the first three years working at the car park Thomas accepted that he could do anything he wanted, given that he remained within the car park in case anything might happen. So, he slept.

Thomas' commute to work was a three-minute walk. For the first three hours Thomas felt groggy after having just woken up. He never drunk caffeinated drinks, only mellow teas or warm milk. And he would sit at the window and look forward over the two barriers into an unchanging grey wall. These first three hours passed quickly. He had never seen someone park or retrieve a car after 10pm or before 5am, but to play it safe he added an hour each way. So, he slept between 11pm and 4am. Sometimes it was a full sleep, still connected to the previous. Other times it was merely a pitiful daydream type sleep, one that sends the imagination into over drive. Such vitality made Thomas mad. Yet he quickly dampened his anger for fear it was wake him up a little too much. Thomas found he could drag the awakening at 4am through to 5am, remaining in a crappy half-sleep and half-life. This left only the remaining two hours to get through. He felt this is how all people must get through their banal, sad and sick lives, metering off hour after hour to this or that quickening abstraction, until you're left solely with the hours you can't avoid.

Those two hours were the lifetime of his day. The time that could not be avoided. The existence that could not be slept. Time, Thomas thought, was a waste. Yes, quite, indeed, time is a waste of time. And left with pure ontological waste, Thomas only sought to use life against life, and spent those two hours going over his notes and double-checking that there wasn't an extra minute he could be sleeping. He had recently shaved his head after a night where a stray hair somehow made him cough himself awake. A triumph.

On average, Thomas estimated, he had been awake—as it is commonly defined—around four hours a day. 10pm-11pm, 5am-7am, with an additional hour added in for variance, inclusive of a lot of half-sleep time that he had been—and still is—working on transforming into full sleep. It appears easy to transform life into sleep, you just have to not be, to not feel, not do. Thomas knew it was actually quite difficult, everything in you, all that life, wants to live, and yet he did not. Thomas found you can't actively not be, you can't try and sleep. Sleep is submission. Death being the mandatory submission, one he revered to such an extent that he felt it, death, had a time and a place for him, and so he did not rush things. For a while he had really forced the sleep. Foods, supplements, medication, auto-hypnosis, drugs, etc. They worked for a while, but the body builds a tolerance. The body wants to be alive and be awake and Thomas didn't want to be alive or be awake. Everything pushed back. But only externally. Internally he found he could just give in. To himself, to sleep, to temporary death, to the abyss, he could just fall into it. Time to sleep, he'd say to himself internally and as if by magic he'd be all dreary and fatigued. Like a lover who has lost their soulmate and is merely biding time, Thomas waited for death, meeting and liaising with it from afar until their righteous reunion.

# The Checkout Woman is Dead

From where I had parked up, in hindsight, I could already see her slumped onto the checkout scanner, but I reacted only by rubbing my face and eyes, shaking my head a little and refusing to look that way any further. And so, I just got out of the car, closed the door brashly, and headed into the shop.

There was a lot of people in the carpark. I saw one man open his car door and vomit onto the tarmac. He was sweaty. He drove off swiftly after catching my eye. He was welling up, I think. I walked into the shop. A big supermarket, the front of which was almost entirely glass and reflected the carpark back upon itself, yet equally allowed one to see the cashiers hard at work, scanning and scanning.

I didn't really know what I wanted from the shop, but I had told myself a fancied a snack and so took that as an excuse to drive the 15 minutes here and avoid doing whatever it was I was doing or should have been doing. I was wandering aimlessly, basically. I knew any sufficient snack would only be within two or three generically high-coloured aisles. I decided on a bag of sweets that was described as 'share size'. I would go on to eat them all and remember not a single flavour. Mastication, much like smoking, is simply pure duration.

I then set out to buy the sweets and swiftly leave. But as I was exiting the aisle I caught sight of the reflection of those front windows, this time reflecting the checkout workers back upon themselves with only a faint image of the cars outside coming through. In the inward reflection, there she was again, a woman sat at the checkout entirely slumped onto the scanner before her, arms dangling heavy by her sides. I walked a little further down the aisle to get a better view of her, perhaps some 20 or 30 feet away.

I held the bag of sweets in my right hand. It somehow kept swinging by my side, banging a little into my leg. I was looking at her slumped over, heavy head and shoulders pooling onto metal. I figured she was passed out, maybe ill or exhausted. But if I had been seeing right as I parked up, then she had been in this state for a few minutes now. Maybe no one had seen her, I thought.

I stepped forward and noticed a man moving towards the till, a few items in his basket ready to be placed. Surely, he would see her and say something. He placed his items on the checkout, at the far end of the conveyor, and they slowly made their way towards the slumped woman. The first item, a large can of soup tapped against her head, falling over and proceeding to roll against the side of her face. As the soup stopped its roll the conveyor equally quit its movement. A few items now lined up before the woman. The customer in question didn't seem, in any sense, to notice her. Stood at the end of the aisle I looked around, maybe trying to get the attention of others. No one noticed me and I can't say I noticed anyone else.

The customer at the till, a late middle-age man with a beer gut and greying hair, was now looking at his phone, scrolling on some app. Occasionally he'd glance outside, but it was clear there was no real reason for this. Some minutes passed and he put his phone away and looked at his shopping. Another customer had arrived, placed a plastic separator on the conveyor, and began to place their items down. They also looked at the woman, and then at the other customer, and then at their shopping. The first customer simply sighed, gave an audible Hmmph and shot a look at the other customer. I still stood at the end of the aisle. The bag of sweets had stopped swinging now.

The first customer, leaning clumsily over the low plastic divider, began to grab his items one by one and, with his gut pressed flat against the clear divide scanned each item through the checkout himself. With the smaller items he managed to avoid contact with the woman, but with the larger items—a pack of loo rolls and a couple of large bottles of soda—he had to push her slumped head out of the way. He didn't touch her with his hands, simply using the soda bottle to force her head to one side. After the checkout beeped and the item had gone through, her head slumped back to its original heavy position. The man then bagged up his things and placed some money from his wallet on the bagging area and then walked away. The next customer was now waiting in front of the clear divider, their items likewise now pushing against the side of the slumped woman's head. A friend of theirs happened to walk by at the end of the till.

Oh, hey Tracy!

Oh my God! How long...it must have been what, three years? How have you been? How are the kids? Are you still down at the Avenue?

Yeah, we're still down there! Kids are okay, though we don't talk to Billy nowadays. Me and Kev are doing fine though he had a hip operation and a triple bypass last year, but that's how life is, you know?

Oh don't I just know it! My Henry had a couple of scares last year and rolled his car. But it's just how it is, isn't it?

This went on for some time and I must admit I was somewhat caught in their talk more than I was the reality of the checkout woman who was still slumped at her till. I actually knew both of the people loosely. One I went to school with and the other cut my hair once ten years ago. That's most of the world though, strange fleeting acknowledgement of something that we didn't notice properly the first time around.

I headed over to the checkout. I would like to say I did so out of some sense of concern, but admittedly I wanted to get home, yet still, the experience was of interest and intrigue.

I grabbed a divider and placed my bag of sweets behind it and stood near the middle of the conveyor, watching as packet of celery pushed its way beneath the slumped woman's hair. Eventually the two friend's chatter ceased, one went on her way, and the other returned to look at her items. She gave me a quick look, let out a sigh, and also began to reach over the divider and push and scan her items passed the slumped woman's head. I watched as one item was removed allowing another to shove itself against the side of her face and hair. The customer leaned far over and grabbed a carrier bag from the stack. Thank you, she said into the air, to no one. She packed up her things and also placed some money on the till. She then walked away with her stuff, looking back and giving me a little nod, perhaps in acknowledgement of the delay.

I removed the divider and watched as my bag of sweets pushed into her hair, the woman still slumped before me. Some of her hair had got caught in the conveyor and was pulled tense against the metal of the checkout. I stood the other side of the plastic divider. I could see all these greasy smears on it which made me frown a little. I leant over with the intention of both picking up my sweets and seeing what was going on. I grabbed the sweets with my left hand and looked over the back of the woman's head. She was all there, a full, human woman, unconscious, perhaps dead. Maybe she was not there I thought to myself. It all felt empty. I grabbed my sweets, pushed the code over the scanner, my finger accidentally caressing her hair. I placed them down and checked my wallet. I didn't have the change. I took my card out of my wallet without thought of what to do.

Do you need a hand, sir?

Excuse me?

Is the card machine not working? Let me get that for you. Without thinking I handed the man my card, and before I thought anything of it he had stepped behind the checkout and was handing the machine over with my card in it. You can enter your pin now. These have been playing up all day!

What about her?

Huh?

Her, I said, gesturing towards the slumped woman.

You just need to do the pin.

I didn't feel well then and so I put in my card pin, grabbed the sweets and began to leave. The other man had left already. I looked back and she was still there, slumped over. I mustn't have been well I thought.

~

If I am honest with myself, I completely forgot about the woman at the checkout very quickly. By the time a day or two had passed thought of that woman didn't even enter my mind. I happened to be away on a work trip for a week, some or other sales event half way up the country. I returned on the Monday after deciding to spend the Sunday away as a short type of break, even if it was followed by a long week of work. I had the Monday off and decided to spend it sorting the house out, restocking necessities, doing all that stuff that has to be done and fills time and next thing you know it you're dying. This entailed a trip to the store. Now, I must admit, at this juncture a memory of the slumped woman did arise in my mind but I hadn't a clue what to do with it. The thought disappeared as soon as I was focused on something else, in this case, getting into to the car to go to the store. It was mid-to-late evening, half-light dreary time.

I parked up and got out. I was checking something on my phone and walking in a half-jog to get inside as there was a slight drizzle of rain. Out of the corner of my eye I acknowledged it intuitively but didn't accept it.

I entered the store and couldn't avoid breaking all social etiquette by halting with a dead stop, slamming without consent into a wall of death scent. Thick pungent rot smell that made a hot jet of thin vomit reach up my throat. When you manage to swallow vomit back down you can always explicitly taste the acid. I placed my face into the back of my elbow, my hand naturally grabbing onto my back for safety. I looked and turned rightward and began marching without any recourse as to just exactly what it was I planned to do.

A few people were queuing for most of the checkouts. Before me four people stood lined up. All there shopping sitting neatly on the conveyor, tucked behind dividers. The person at the front of the queue was leaning over the divider as I had done just over a week ago. I walked up and pushed myself between them and the next customer. The stench of the dead cashier penetrating all cloth. Nose dribbling, eyes running, throat contracting and lightly launching acid belch upwards, some of which I had to spit into my sleeve.

Looking down over the divider I saw her once again, yet so much gone. Her hair had been consistently caught and chunked out by the conveyor, with little pieces of rotting scalped lined up along the metal. Her eye-socket was empty with the ball itself turned to a black mulch, all spilled over everything. Looking further down and I saw that her body was thin and her clothes draped off her and her shoes had fallen off and there was faeces and flesh and fluid on the floor.

Excuse me Sir! No need to push in!

Yeah, mate, there's a queue here!

The first customer scanned another item. Pushing a packet of instant noodles passed the dead woman's face, grazing her and leaving a gaping wound that spilled a thin yellow grease onto the scanner. I looked forward to the next checkout. The woman there was sat up and scanning the customer's items, making inaudible conversation. She looked at me and nothing of her face or person changed when she did so.

I took my arm away from my face as to proclaim aloud that the cashier woman was dead, but as I did so the smell hit the back of my throat and filled my mouth and I vomited hot half-digested pastry onto the floor. It landed with a slap. The manager appeared once again.

Everything okay sir? Do you need to sit down? Need me to call someone?

That woman, I said, trying not to vomit anymore, on the checkout. She is dead.

You have been sick on the floor. I think if you're not feeling well, you should get home, sir.

The woman. She is rotting.

I think you should head off now sir.

# The Cruise

We won! We won! shrieked the wife into the phone.

Oh my God! Are you serious? replied the husband.

Yes! They just called to confirm it with me! We won! We won! yelled the wife whilst nudging their dog away with her foot. The husband stood in the middle of his communal work office, shouting to be heard and yet attempting to appear humble. This is incredible! The most prestigious and elusive cruise known to man!

...it's as if he's repeating the adverts word-for-word, quipped a fatigued colleague out of the corner of his mouth. Something the husband noticed, noted, and subconsciously knew he would enact revenge for at a later date in some banal act of bureaucratic passive aggression. Sorry for yelling guys, but you'll never guess what?

You're going on the cruise?

Oh my, sorry, yes, you must have overheard. I'm ever so sorry about that. But yes! Yes! We're going on the cruise!

~

They met at a work party when they were in their mid-20s. It was a party, everyone knew it was a party, but both of them called it a 'work function' all night. Very few people liked them, very few people hated them, and if they knew just how many people didn't think of them at all they would surely both commit suicide. They may not have ended up together, but they did, and so that's how it is now. He moved into her place quickly after they started dating. In terms of values, they had little in common because neither of them had any actual values. Though neither was ever to admit such, their lives bent to the whim of whatever might gain them status or favour within the eyes of others, and, as the majority of people acted also in such a way, the case is such that all act as if watched by an elusive no one who never appears, never is, and never was. And so all obey the all that is not. They liked going to the popular restaurants. They watched the latest popular films (nothing too pretentious). They went on cruises multiple times a year. Outside of this they would take city breaks and glamping trips. Everyone knew where they went and what they did because where they went and what they did was made known to everyone by their repetitive announcements, both overt and covert. They had decided not to have children, with neither of them wishing to accept that this was due to their desire to live continually as they always have done. This decision led them to get a dog because that's what people do. They have a hot-tub and two spare rooms. He 'likes' jazz. She 'likes' olives. They do a lot of other stuff and own a lot of other things. None of it matters. Some would say that what one saw of their social media was in fact a lie, and that in truth it was merely hand-picked moments as to curate the image of the perfect modern life. Others would state that perhaps they were just happy doing what they do and who were we to judge. Some would think and believe their lives were perfect. Others would think and believe their lives were a lie. The truth was not in-between (as usually is the case), this couple were exactly as vapid and shit-eating as they made themselves appear to be.

~

The adverts were everywhere. A cruise simply known as The Cruise, hosted by an unnamed company, promised a cruise of infinite possibility and desire. It was understood that the company understood desire greater than all. A ship that supposedly sailed just beyond the heart, waiting for it to catch up and claim that which all along it was rightly owed. One could not buy a ticket. There was no sales team. No website or contact information. A holiday so perfect they contacted you. There were forums dedicated to ship sightings and rumours of onboard proceedings. There was no truth to anything anyone had said of The Cruise who had not themselves been invited aboard, and, as it was, all of those invited aboard had remained entirely silent of their experience.

~

They received a further call the morning after the first call that consisted solely of a date and a time in the unspoken understanding that they, the company, already knew their address and that was perfectly fine, and that they, the husband and wife, would be ready to go at the given date and time. The husband and wife had already packed all the predictable, asinine, and inane detritus modern people consider to be essential four days before the boarding procedure was even to begin. Each night they cooked a special meal and grinned at each other with such transparent smugness that their dog found them to be strangers, and, as such, growled at them and cowered outside.

The day arrived and neither the husband nor the wife could contain themselves. He sat in the lounge listening to a record people pretend to like and she pretended to tidy up and message friends, but both their minds were focused solely on The Cruise. Their dog was nowhere to be found.

A limousine with blacked out windows pulled up and the husband and wife were quick to grab their suitcases and head outside. The front door closed behind them and clicked shut as to signify it was locked, but both were beyond the front gate before the sound had time to register. They stood side by side in front of the limousine and nothing happened. He turned to look at her and gave an awkward smirk, she leant forward and looked intently at the driver's window. It lowered by an inch. Get in, said an empty voice. They got in, awkwardly dragging their suitcases through the door.

The instant they sat down the limousine took off at quite a pace. Blimey! said the wife. The husband laughed. She looked at him in annoyance. There was a single light inside the limousine, at the other end, and so they sat in a dull static light that sought only to depress. The husband felt around and looked at things with a critical gaze. The leather of the seats was frayed. There were two small water bottles rolling around on the floor. How long until we get there? said the wife loud enough for whoever was driving to hear. No one replied.

The driving wasn't erratic or forceful, but merely determined and precise. The husband and wife could not see outside of the windows. The husband needed to urinate. He slid to the front and tapped on the blacked-out divider glass between their section and the unknown driver's. Excuse me, said the husband, how long until we get there, a little embarrassing, but I need to use the loo. Still no reply.

A few moments later the limousine came to a clear stop. Are we here? said the wife. Who cares, said the husband, I gotta pee. He left everything behind and quickly got out. The sun hurt his eyes but he saw enough to notice that they were at a port. The limousine was in a wide-open space. A gate could be seen a long way away and everything not open to the sea was protected by high razor-wire fencing. He jogged to the fencing some 40 meters away leaving the limousine behind him. The wife proceeded to exit the limousine to have a look around. The husband started to pee. Say, where are we? asked the wife. The limousine drove off, the wife yelled after it, it took an unseen rightward turn and disappeared. The husband jogged back over. Did they just drive off with our suitcases?

Yes! She looked at his unwashed hands and rolled her eyes.

Well, what are we going to do?

Let's head over to the ship, I'm sure there's been a mistake.

Okay, he said, as a little bit or leftover urine fell out of the tip of his penis and dribbled down his leg.

~

Before the husband and wife sat the ship that was to take them on The Cruise. It looked like a cruise ship in form, yet, there was not a single signifying feature, name, nor blemish. It stood, from every angle, as a shape of matt white flat against the horizon. As they looked it over the excitement of The Cruise returned to them and they turned to one another and, forgetting their suitcase dilemma, hugged without clasping or kissing. The husband let out a sigh of odd relief and the wife rearranged her dress.

You must be the winners?

A man had appeared behind them. He was stood absolutely vertical, not a single joint out of place, it was clear he knew not what it meant to slouch. He wore a white uniform bereft of all embellishments or markings, inclusive of a plain white cap. His eyes pierced the husband and wife at the same time, a shimmering cyan coming into you, and a nice white grin with lips that lagged behind calculated thought.

Hello? said the wife clasping the husband's arm.

I'm guessing you're with The Cruise? said the husband clasping the wife's arm.

Yes, I am. I am here to onboard you.

What does that involve? said the wife.

Getting you onboard. Come on now, follow me.

~

The husband and wife followed the uniformed man as he walked toward the ship at a perfectly straight line from where they had previously stood. As they approached the immense whiteness of the ship a black opening slowly appeared in its side and, jutting out from it, a gangway, the shadows of which were its only determining factor. An infolded whiteness with but a single black rectangle for entry. The uniformed man stood at the start of the gangway and, acting as if he had never met neither the husband or wife before now, greeted them. Hello Sir, Madam.

May I welcome you to The Cruise, we were, of course, expecting you.

Of course. The limousine drove off with our-

Madam, Sir, could I ask you to please proceed onboard, we haven't much time.

Our cases?

It's just up the gangway, he said, gesturing towards the matt black entryway.

Without questioning they continued a movement that felt halted and headed up the gangway. Halfway along the husband looked back to the uniformed man who was stood at the very end of the gangway, directly in the middle, looking up at them with intent. The husband put his hand on the wife's shoulder, I'm sure they'll sort our cases, he said, not believing his own words. They approached the doorway and swiftly entered, their legs being encased in a cool shadow as they both stepped in. Looking around into a dull, indiscernible static metal room, they knew not what to do nor where to go. The wife looked out of the entryway and down the gangway. Excuse me, she mildly shouted to the uniformed man, but where do we go...what do we do?

Just close the door for now, he said.

The wife nudged the husband out of the way and proceeded to close the heavy metal door. The husband instinctively helped her and, before they knew it, it was closed and they were in. There was a click of metal from inside the door, yet no lights came on and nothing happened. The husband looked out of the small circular window within the door, once again peering down the gangway, tapping at the glass, trying to get the uniformed man's attention. The husband was overtly gesturing the words What do we do? Where do we go? with his lips. The uniformed man looked up at them and gave the slightest bow before he yanked the gangway away, causing it to fall between the boat and the dock, crashing against concrete, metal, and sea. What was that? said the wife alarmingly. That man...he just pulled the gangway away and it fell, I think it must have been a mistake? The husband then overtly mouthed the words Are you okay? to the uniformed man. He, the uniformed man, was folding his little white hat which he then proceeded to place in his pocket. He stepped towards to the edge of the dock and, with eyes glazed over, fell forward, stiff as a plank into the gap. He didn't make a sound. Oh my God! yelled the husband.

What? What is it?

That man! The one in the uniform! He just fell in!

What?!

Come on we have to get someone!

~

The husband and wife found themselves within a small metal space lit only from the light of the small round window. The husband instinctively took his smartphone out from his pocket and turned on the torch. Thick white paint coated all the bolts and metal in the spaces he managed to light. The wife was banging against various walls and beams that jutted out from the sides. Hello! she half-yelled, making a noticeable attempt to laugh off her minor fear. They were there, in that room, for some time.

With a jolt and a distant muffled metallic sound, the ship began to move. The wife, now sat down in the dark with her back against a wall she did not know, lurched forward a little. The husband, face close to the glass of the window, smeared his nose along it. For fucks sake, he said under his breath. At that moment a door at one end of the room, that for lack of light they had not been able to see, unlocked and swung wide with a hideous bang as it hit the wall. Quick! Hold it, I don't want to be stuck in here any longer, the wife said to the husband as she quickly leapt to her feet. The husband strode to the door and held it ajar with his arm, peering onward down a hallway without seeming definition. Here we are, at last, the wife said.

Yes, said the husband feeling quite sick.

As they both stepped forward into the ship the husband let go of the door and it stayed exactly where he had held it and there wasn't a sound and no one was in the corridor and there was nothing to do.

~

What do we do? the wife said to no one.

I don't know, the husband replied to no one.

Before them was set a corridor that appeared to stretch the length of the ship, but that was a distance they did not know. Not a jot of colour but white, barring the carpet which was a faint, patterned blue. The air smelt slightly of sulphur, as if one had just opened a new book or packet of ham. The ceiling was low and curved. Two planes, one white and one blue, with nothing in-between to hold onto. The ship was moving. The wife walked forward a few steps ahead of the husband and looked back at him. She was confused. He looked back at her. He was confused. Both were uncertain of it all.

Come on, he said let's move on a bit and see if can find someone.

What else can we do? she said.

They walked along the corridor for a while and found nothing to look at nor truly perceive. Both the husband and wife routinely stopped to look closely at the paintwork, checking that it had texture. Once the husband even knelt to make sure the carpet was made of anything at all. They had not been walking long and yet for both it felt like quite a while. How long have we been walking? the husband asked. I was just about to ask you the same question replied the wife. Both were useless with regard to their questions.

They came to a door on the righthand side of the corridor. So nestled into the whiteness that both almost missed it. But with a glance backward the wife noticed a slight shadow against the white and quickly stepped back along her path. Look, she said to her husband, who, due to his utter boredom had already noticed her difference and was also quickly to the door. It was blue. One or two shades off from the carpet, with a round metal handle. Without hesitation the wife turned the handle and pushed forward. Nothing. She then turned the handle and pulled backward. Nothing. Give it here, the husband said. He then repeated the same process. Nothing. He then turned the handle and pushed forward harder. Nothing. Then backwards harder. Nothing. The wife glared at him. What? he said. They stood for some time looking it over and wandering what to do. Let's just keep going, the wife said as she marched quicker down the corridor. Behind her she heard a bang, and then another, and another. She turned to see the husband charging the door with his shoulder. He stopped and looked down the corridor to the wife. She turned back and continued down the corridor. He followed.

After a while their legs ached and they grew tired. I honestly think I need to sit down, this is ridiculous!

Me too. We must have missed something.

We didn't miss anything.

With that they both sat down. The husband taking off his jumper and placing it behind his head for support.

You smell like urine, she said.

You know I couldn’t find anywhere to go.

With that they both fell asleep.

~

Morning, said a man in a clean white suit looking down upon the husband and wife.

Excuse me? the husband said bleary eyed.

I said Morning, Sir. As in Good morning.

Huh?

Were your rooms not to your liking?

We got stuck in this corridor all...night?

It seems so. We’re always here to help.

We saw no one!

You got onboarded, yes?

Oh, yes, that man, I need to tell you, I think he fell in.

Could be.

...could be?

I will show you to your rooms. Come with me.

The wife, overlooking the conversation, quickly jumped to her feet. Excuse me, sir! But we've been sleeping here, in this...corridor, all night! I think you owe us an apo-

The man in the white suit turned and looked at her and she felt hollow and empty and ill. He turned away. Come along now. He quickly began walking back along the corridor, from the direction the husband and wife had come from. Excuse me, we've been walking down there all night and couldn't see-

It's right here, the man in the white suit pronounced loudly. Some 30 or so meters away he held open a door and gestured into it. The wife looked at the husband and they both felt odd. They walked over to the man and looked into the room and then back at the man. The husband physically shuddered and then smiled Not sure how we missed this last night. Anyway, our luggage got taken by the-

All in order sir, don't worry. Enjoy your room.

Okay, that's great. Thank you.

With that the husband walked into the room and the wife followed. Before them were two small single beds, a small bedside table, a lamp, and a thin rug. The room was noticeably small, without a single window. There was a bathroom off to the right with a shower, toilet, and sink. Everything was suspiciously and uncannily clean. Excuse me, the wife said, I think there must be-she turned back to the man in the white suit and he was gone. She checked the corridor and he wasn't there.

He's gone, the wife said, looking back to the husband.

Gone where? the husband said, walking over to the door.

I don't know.

He must be...the husband leant out of the door, looking down each direction of the corridor, ...huh. He looked at her and she at him.

Look, let's take a shower and then take a look around afterwards, okay?

Sure.

They got undressed, throwing their things onto their respective beds before heading into the shower. The water was lukewarm and it made their skin quickly prune. They tried kissing in the shower, the water splashing over them, but it wasn't hot enough for comfort, and the kiss didn't connect and they both felt the reality of the other's flesh that they didn't know all that well. They looked at each other and knew that in time it wouldn't last but for now there was enough there for a modicum of normality.

After the shower they quickly dried off and sat naked opposite each other on their respective beds. The husband looked away from the wife at part of the wall where he'd imagined a window or balcony would have been, staring out to a sea he wasn't sure he was on. The wife's skin had gone all dry. I don't have my creams, she said, accepting that she wouldn't be getting them.

Oh, the husband replied. Do you know what time it is?

No.

Me neither.

Shall we take a nap?

We just slept.

Oh, yeah. Shall we head out, then?

I guess so.

Where should we go?

I don't know.

What do we do?

What is there to do?

Nothing, it seems.

Okay. Let's head out.

They put their clothes on, quickly turning away from one another as they did so.

~

The husband stood up first, pushing off his bed slowly and stepping to the cabin door. Looking back at the wife he thought she seemed older, then he thought that if she knew what he was thinking she would be angry with him. The wife pushed off her bed thinking nothing at all. The husband opened the door and stepped out into the same corridor as before. It's the same, he said over his shoulder.

Well, I guess it would be.

Okay, come on.

Okay.

She watched as his shoulder disappeared round the corner and followed him out of the door and she looked to the left and he was gone and he looked behind him and she was gone. Both went to say something, both already felt tired, both went in separate directions. He wanted something to eat. She wanted to find their luggage. They both walked for some time. Occasionally they would both stop, he more often than her, she flipping between fury and betrayal and sadness, him between hunger and annoyance and frustration. In time he came to a door and she to an expanse.

The husband pushed open the door and found what appeared to be a canteen. A long row of serving hatches shot down the left-hand side. All their shutters were closed. The rest of the room was filled with tables and chairs set out in a horrid symmetry.

The wife continued on down a corridor that at once opened into a large room of nothing lined by white walls and a wooden floor. As she looked back the corridor was gone and she stood in the centre of the glossed shine.

He banged on the shutters.

She walked and leant against the wall.

Some more time passed, as it always does.

~

Eventually he sat at one of the tables closest to the shutters and placed his head in his hands. The wife stood and walked to the side of the room and leant with her back against the immaculate white wall, bowing her chin to her chest, and shuffling her feet aimlessly.

Everything okay there, Sir? said a steward of the ship, clad in white and white with a little gold embroidery.

Sorry? the husband said, looking from his hands.

Is everything okay? If I may say so Sir, you look a tad exhausted, distraught, even?

The husband attempted to get himself together and felt he was tired of it all and all other things too and yet he'd never admit this. Yes, everything is all good. Any chance of some food? I hadn't noticed, but I'm quite hungry actually.

Of course, Sir, anything else?

You haven't seen my wife around, have you?

Ah, the wife! Yes, yes. I saw her some time ago. She was having quite the time.

How do I get to her?

I'll just be back with the food for you sir.

He sat and looked over the table at more tables and chairs just like his own. Nothing to them. They were entirely pragmatic and they inspired no thoughts in him at all. Soon enough the steward returned with his food. A chicken soup, a cheese sandwich, and a glass of water. He placed them on the table in front of the husband. Thank you, Sir.

I'm not too keen on-, but the steward was gone. And yet he still wasn't keen on either chicken soup or cheese sandwiches, but he didn't hate them either, they would do for now. He ate them slowly, often using his back teeth to chew as to avoid the taste, maybe he was bored he thought to himself.

The wife remained leant against the wall. After some time, she shifted her back down the wall so it was like she was sat on an invisible chair. Then she would stand up again. A steward entered from somewhere she couldn't discern, as if appearing from in between the light and the white walls. Everything okay?

I'm not sure.

Oh, said the steward looking right at her from some 20 feet away, the light illuminating all of him in two-dimensions only.

Well, it's just...what is there to do here?

People used to dance here.

Dance?

Yes.

People?

Yes. But they don't anymore.

Oh.

They don't dance anymore.

I see.

Would you like to dance, Miss?

Is there any music? We could I guess-

Oh, no. Not with me. I meant, would you like to dance, generally speaking.

Do you mean do I like to dance?

No, I don't! I mean what I say. Would you like to dance?

In the future?

Yes.

I've never thought about it specifically. It's just something that you do at certain events, isn't it?

I don't know, is it?

I think so.

Okay.

Could you take me somewhere where I can get some food, I'm really quite hungry.

Of course, Miss. Follow me.

And so, she followed the steward who appeared to flux in and out of her vision. His outline seeping into the white walls of the room, and then a corridor, and then another large white room, and then another corridor that to her felt very long, and then finally the canteen. Here you are Miss, the steward said.

I'm technically Mrs, not Miss-

But the steward had faded away, or gone somewhere that she had missed. She looked around and only just managed to catch her husband sat at a table. He was out of focus. Blending into the room. Hunched over a bowl.

~

But you don't like chicken soup?

No.

Or cheese sandwiches?

It's what they gave me. Are you going to sit down?

Okay. How did you find this place?

Not sure. You?

Steward brought me here. I was in some dance hall.

Dance hall? The steward said you were having a good time!

No. I wasn't. I was just there and the steward said they used to dance there. Listen, I'm really tired.

Here you are Miss! said the steward as he placed down a tomato soup and a corned beef sandwich with a glass of water.

Thank you, she said automatically but the steward was gone.

You hungry?

I should be, but this doesn't look like anything.

No, and I can't really taste mine.

And they sat and ate their soups and sandwiches for a long time and every now and again one of them would look around, sometimes even twisting their head behind them to see if anything was happening, but it wasn't. Sometimes he would look at her. Sometimes she would look at him. When they looked at each other there was nothing to say.

After they'd finished their meals neither felt full nor empty. They sat at the table for some time, not looking or seeing, not really being, but they were there and they had no choice in that. They had no say in it, they had to exist.

Come on, the husband said, let's get back to the room.

How do we get there?

Don't know. Let's just start off in some direction.

Okay.

It was silent. The type of silence that allows you to hear the shifting of clothes or deep breathes, the type of silence where when all is stopped you notice a faint buzzing coming from the air itself, as if behind it were something that had your strings. They listened to the steps of their feet for a while. Then quickly turned a corner and found themselves back at their cabin.

Ah! You found your way back okay then? said the steward who stood to the right of their cabin door.

I guess we did.

Well, here you are, so you did indeed!

What do we do?

I'm sorry, Sir?

What is there to do?

I don't fully understand?

What...activities, events...stuff, things...what is there to do!

Excuse me Miss, I don't fully understand the husband, could you explain?

Entertainment or something like that I think he's on about.

I'm really sorry, I don't quite know what it is you need?

A fucking TV, anything!

A fucking TV, Sir?

Sorry for that. Mind your language!

Oh, forget it!

Well, I shall leave you both to it. I hope you get a good night's sleep.

~

They walked into the cabin one after another, a prison line of two people. They sat across from each other on their beds, holding their heads slightly bowed, with nothing to say and not a memory between them. Everything was still. For a while they sat looking down at the floor, and then at their feet, and then upwards at the wall, and then back down.

What should we do? one of them said to the other.

I don't know, the other replied.

~

And it was that the husband and the wife sat on the ship for quite some time. Occasionally one would venture out of the cabin and return sometime later. Occasionally the other would do the same. Hours and days blended together and they passed one another in an empty haze. They slept a lot. When they were awake, they couldn't grasp onto anything for comfort. At one point the husband mentioned something from a time passed to the wife and she simply replied Don't and they never spoke of anything outside of the ship again. Soon enough they couldn't be together and the trips outside of the cabin became longer. He had become fond of a room he found that he had named 'The Nest'. It was a small, 10ft by 10ft room which had a few pieces of straw strewn over the floor. The husband liked the straw. She had become fond of a corridor she liked to call 'The Runway'. It seemingly went on forever and she liked to run as fast as she could down it bare foot, sometimes screaming, sometimes crying, sometimes both.

How was the Nest? she would ask.

It was quiet again, he would reply

Yes.

And how about you, how is the Runway?

Oh yes, I run a lot.

Very good.

One time the wife had run so fast down the Runway that she became top heavy and entered into a forward gallop destined for the floor. And that destiny did meet her and the wife, one time, smashed her face into the floor so hard she dislodged a molar and grazed the entire left side of her head. On returning to the husband that one time he said Did the runway get you? looking into the floor. And she didn't reply because she was crying and the tears were making her cuts sting. She wasn't mad at him. Maybe she didn't care, maybe she did. But she knew what the Nest was, she'd found it one time when aimlessly walking around the ship. This is his Nest, she thought to herself when she found it. She looked around and saw the straw had been arranged neatly in height order, she was not surprised. Then she turned and saw a white sock almost standing on end, soaked and crusted with semen, she was not surprised. And so, when her tears stung her cuts, the thought of the husband running away to jerk off in his tiny Nest soothed the empty pain.

~

They spent a few nights together in the cabin. Both there. But this became potent, sordid, a state that bordered on confusion. They couldn't do it even if they did. Even in sleep the tension kept them awake and both arose utterly exhausted with only the other to blame. Waking up every day with an excuse, that's Eden. The time went on, as it tends to do. And they sat in silence, as they tended to do.

~

Soon enough a steward arrived at their cabin and informed them that they would be docking soon, and to have their belongings ready to go within the hour. Both had just awoken after an indeterminate sleep, bleary eyed and half-weeping. Both sat up onto the edge of their respective beds, almost as if they mirrored one another. The wife looked up at the husband. The husband looked up at the wife. And, both looked through each other and the fatigue had its say. The husband laid back down on the bed and the wife stood up, waiting.

~

Soon enough the steward again returned. Excuse me, but the ship is set to leave again in 15 minutes, I believe we did inform you we were docking some hours ago. If you would care to follow me.

Oh, sure, said the husband.

Our belongings? said the wife.

They are right there. Now, come along.

The wife looked down and saw their suitcases. She picked hers up automatically, as did the husband. They both followed the steward with the wife taking the lead.

Sorry to rush you, the steward said, but I am sure we told you we would be arriving soon!

No, it's okay-

Here we are! announced the steward before the original door they had entered in from some time ago. The gangplank before them stretched out to the place where they had been dropped off. Well, it has been a pleasure! said the steward.

Yes, said the wife.

Bye, said the husband.

And with that they both set down the gangplank and toward a waiting car. They placed their luggage in the boot and got inside. The husband slept. The wife looked out of the window. Soon enough they were home and automatically got out of the car and grabbed their stuff. They got the key from under the mat, stepped inside, and locked the door behind them. I'm going to bed, the husband said.

Okay, said the wife.

As the husband walked up the stairs the wife checked the calendar. It had been two weeks. She unpacked their things and instinctively threw much of it into the bin. The rest went into the wash. Soon enough she found herself on the sofa sleeping.

~

She was awoken by the sound of paws on the wooden floor. Little scratches without any other sound. She opened her eyes and found their dog looking at her vacant yet hungry. She got up and poured some dog biscuits into a bowl, placed the packet back, and then returned to the sofa. She wondered who had fed their dog. She went out the back door and stood on her tiptoes to check if the neighbours were there. They were. They caught her looking.

Oh my god! You're back! I thought I heard something! I'll come over, you must tell me everything!

...Oh, very soon Jill, very soon! But we're both so tired. I just came to say-

Thank you for feeding the dog? Yes, not at all, not at all. We lobbed a few leftovers over and it rained a fair bit, but I bet she's doing great.

She looks great, thank you Jill! As I say, very tired, but we can chat tomorrow maybe. Back to work tomorrow!

Oh yes, yes. How silly of me! Well, I'll catch you tomorrow.

The wife felt a surge of energy within her as she closed the back door. The dog came up to her, already finishing the bowl of food, the wife nudged it away with her foot. She walked away without looking and went to bed.

~

Morning love! the husband said.

Good morning! the wife said.

Can't wait for work.

Oh?

Well, surely you can't wait to tell everyone about the Cruise?

I know, I know, it's going to be amazing!

They got ready as they always had done. She put on a jazz record. He took ages to make a coffee that tasted like burnt shit. Soon enough they were ready and got in their respective cars and went their respective ways.

~

Well, obviously I can't say too much as you all know they're very secretive...but...oh my god, the pool...I just can't...the food...I can't even explain to you about the food, it was just, better than anything I've ever eaten. I'm not sure food will ever be the same for me...the staff were impeccable, incredible, truly...I can't for the life of me think of anything even close to negative to say about it...the ship itself? Glorious. Not huge. But...something about it just makes you feel at home and new and...oh I just can't...I'll tell you more about it over lunch...I'll tell you more about it over lunch...so good to be back in a way though...so good to be back in a way though!

~

When the husband got home from work, he opened the front door, stepped into the house, locked the door behind him and placed his coat on its peg. As he leant down to untie his shoes the dog leapt at him from behind and sunk its teeth into his upper thigh and ass, ripping the flesh through the trousers. The force of the hit made the husband fall into the wall and bang his head, knocking him unconscious. The dog continued tearing the flesh from his thigh. Blood pissing all over everything. The dog's face glorious and enraged.

~

When the wife returned home, she opened the front door and saw the husband lying on the floor and quickly shoved the door open and fell down to her knees beside him. Oh my god! Are you okay? What the fuck! she looked him over and noticed all the blood everywhere. She looked at the blood on the wooden floor and thought that if the blood had been soaking here long enough the boards might need replacing due to damp. The dog leapt at her neck, severed a vital artery and walked off with a strange piece of meaty sinew hanging from its mouth.

# A gentle light all made of blue

If you could tell us about the night?

The night?

Vision? I think it's been given many names.

Ah, I see. I'm sure I can think back, I was cycling home from the shop...there were two slight hills, almost unnoticeable unless one had a backpack full of stuff slowing them down, weighing them down, which I did quite often back then-

What day was this?

I can't remember what day it was exactly, perhaps a Monday? No, a Tuesday? Though it could have been Wednesday, no, definitely Tuesday...of course, because I would have been returning from Mass.

Did you go to Mass often?

I went when I could back then, but living in the countryside you were lucky for a Mass once a week so you seized what you could. Actually, that's unfair, we had about four Masses per week and one was on a Tuesday evening, around 7pm.

What was your faith like then?

What is one's faith like at any point?

I wouldn't know.

Not a believer?

I'm a neutral party.

Well, back then I hadn't been in a while, if I remember right, and we had confession beforehand on a Tuesday and, yes, I would have been very nervous you know. Because, well, if you've ever been to confession, I can only say that sometimes it's like chatting about a spreadsheet of awkward facts and other times you're more vulnerable than you've ever been.

You know all this quite vividly, it seems?

Maybe. Confession is very personal; you remember most of them. As you can imagine I have recalled that night many times. But memories are only memories of memories, as I'm sure you know. But anyway, you must understand all of this was very long ago, quite some time now, to the degree that it's like a pure memory, like it just is and I haven't any say in it.

Do you happen to remember the exact date?

Oh, sure, I could likely find you a date and perhaps even a time, but that's not the point. Do you see what I mean?

So, what was the date?

I would prefer not to.

No?

To be honest, without sounding rude, I think you could quite easily figure out the date and time and all that jazz without my help. I'm sure you have the details, but that's not why you're here.

I understand, so what were you doing at this point in your life?

Thank you. I was sort of doing this and that. I had a main job at the time, but it never felt full, like I could go do what I wanted really. Sure, I had to spend a lot of my week on it like most people, but when I worked the time just disappeared and it was everything else that remained. I imagine that after sleep, work, eating, and all that, only about 1/100th of any single person's life is in any sense meaningful, if that. But it's odd, mostly I remember a lot of cycling back then. I was very into fitness of any kind that worked.

That worked?

Well, I was drinking a lot beforehand, like years before, and then I stopped, and started, and stopped...you get the picture. And so, fitness becomes your other addiction, but you can't keep up a fitness...a fitness, a sport, whatever, that you aren't keen on.

So, cycling you were keen on?

Yes. Lots of cycling. Some lifting. That was the bulk of it. Some stretching or callisthenic type stuff. We're sort of going off track, aren't we?

Depends. What did you expect from this?

Well, I expected you'd want to know about what I saw that night.

Sure, in time.

Okay.

Were you happy back then?

Happy?

Yes.

What can one really say of happiness? Once I came of age, so to speak, I was utterly disinterested in the idea of happiness that was sold to me. I mean, if happiness is holidays, coffee shops, and a bigger TV, then give me abject misery. I still stand by that.

Were you happy in a different sense, then?

I'm still not sure what happiness in the real sense people talk about is. I've certainly seen it. People who really wanted children and got children and they have those moments, seaside trips and the like, that's happiness. But then equally, I feel I should add that those who really wanted kids and didn't get them, when they go to the seaside, that is unhappiness. Maybe I was too afraid to feel either. I don't know.

So, you weren't happy?

No. No I wasn't.

Have you ever been happy?

I don't think so, no. I mean, it's like love, if you have to think about it then you haven't had it.

Maybe.

Maybe. Have you ever been happy?

Yeah.

See.

Ha. Have you ever been unhappy?

Absolutely.

And that abides by the same rules as happiness for you?

How so?

Well, you didn't have to think about it...

Yeah. Same rules. Ever been unhappy?

Now and again.

Now and again isn't unhappiness. Not really.

Are you gatekeeping unhappiness?

You'd be surprised, those of us who have made a friend of misery are suspicious of those who only pretend to know it.

It?

Yeah, misery is neutral. We're really off track here.

You want to talk about the night?

Okay.

To draw some of these threads together, did anything change after that night?

You mean in terms of happiness etc.?

Yeah.

No.

No?

It took me a long while to accept that, but no, nothing changed. Something changed somewhere else, that's perhaps the only way I can put it.

Somewhere else?

Yeah, somewhere else.

Could I go back a little?

Sure.

Were you depressed? Back then, that is.

What do you think?

What does my response matter?

You'd be surprised. Never met a depressive who'd truly be able to admit of themselves. Or at least articulate it. Maybe that's right, I don't know.

Were you?

By all normal measures and ideas and all that...yes, yes I was.

And now?

Yeah, still depressed. I'm still depressed. Why?

Why what?

Why does it matter if I was, or am, depressed?

Just wondering.

That night was different, if it matters.

How so?

Hard to explain to someone who hasn't been there. You ever experienced migraines?

A few times, sure.

How long did they go on for?

A few days, longest was about 10 days, actually, now I think on it.

You ever have one stop whilst you're awake?

The euphoria?

Euphoria. Perfect description too, isn't it?

Absolutely.

Well, as far as I'm concerned, the same thing exists with depression except it's far more...unheard of, and one is rarely awake for it, or even conscious of it. And even when it does happen it can just as easily fall into a full-blown mania, other side of the spectrum type thing.

Right?

But once in a while it can...let up. And it's like that euphoria with migraines, kind of, you don't get that odd buzz and it isn't necessarily pleasurable. But something clears, even for just an hour, a few minutes, and that's enough. It's like you've been breathing through a straw for a week and you get a few proper breaths at the weekend. I'm not doing it justice. I can't do it justice.

Respite?

Rest.

Ah.

What we would all give for a single day of actual rest.

So, that night was actual rest?

Shouldn't have been.

Oh?

Like I said at the start, I was cycling over those two hills. I was fairly out of breath. I shouldn't have felt like that. No, I shouldn't have.

So where were you?

Nearing the top of the second hill.

And no one else was around?

Not a soul. I was all alone.

And then?

What I mentioned just now, with depression, the let up, like a break.

A break?

Yeah, a little gentle rupture, maybe.

You were...?

Yes, yes. At the top of the hill, then the sky fell, everything was light, and thinking back it was as if the backpack has ceased to exist and my bike would carry me where I needed it to. It was like 7:30 getting on for 8 by then, deep twilight, people should have been around and yet no one was. I remember looking it up the next morning, but there were no local events or anything, I was just given this space to be for some time.

And that's when you saw her?

I've never said it in such clear terms.

Neither did I.

If anyone overheard this, they would think you were referring to something very clear.

But you did?

I stopped at the top of the hill. Not something I ever would have done, not then, a few blind turns on that road and rural drivers are lazy, ignorant. But I stopped. Top of the second hill, I stopped.

Why?

Blue. Light blue. Light blue coming from the field to my left. A gentle light all made of blue. It shouldn't have been there. It was late. Nearing dark. There's no lights in the countryside anyway. But it was there and I breathed for the first time.

Breathed?

I'm not one for emotion, not at all. I can only relay this by thinking back to being a child, would that be okay?

Okay.

You remember that sadness you felt as a child. Maybe the world was unfair, something didn't go your own way, or you were just upset because that's how childhood is. But you've told yourself you have to keep it together and maybe you're getting told off, maybe you're trembling, maybe even your legs are shaking, but as long as you don't breathe everything will be fine because if you don't breathe the tears don't come. But everyone has to breathe, don't they? Everyone has to breathe. And so, you've held your breath for so long the next breath is a big gasp and it just sends you into floods of tears. And no one likes tears because no one can control them nor the faces they bring to the surface. Scrunched anguish, misery, pain, fear, all of it. And you're crying and you're just absolutely helpless, because that's what tears are, they are this horrid acceptance. But that big breath, in retrospect, it's just great, really cathartic, beautiful, even. I think the universe will end in crying. Crying is the final act. The final misery, a pleading that knows it's run out of all chances.

That's how you felt that night?

Wouldn't do it justice. Some of it was that. You want me to continue?

Okay.

That gentle light flooded into all things. Not over them or shadowing them, it was just them where they were as if everything as it was now was fine, and maybe we all just needed to wait. The road was lit in blue and the grass around held itself aloft and I remember trying to breath and much like what I said about childhood as I took a small breath my face weakened and I began to weep. I brought my hands from the bar of the bike and found my rucksack gone. I stood looking forward and then my bike was gone too. I could feel the tears, they were warm, loving, like nothing I've ever felt.

Like?

Nothing I've ever felt. I cannot do any of this justice. People always ask what are someone's regrets, you know? Mine will be that I cannot relay this to anyone. I feel nothing but anguish at the fact I cannot articulate this.

I'm sorry. Do try.

Yes, yes, I am sorry too. There I stood, at the top of the second hill. No bike now, I was so light, and the tears had stopped, though my eyes did simply well and well. Like someone had shown me a home I never knew I had. Can you imagine that, can you? A life without love or hope or happiness but a single moment gives glimpse to a home and a love abound that you couldn't imagine. I turned to the light and everything was as it will always be and the light held all acceptance true so that peace could find its place. And I turned the final turn, the final step, I was in the field to the left of where I had been riding, grass to my knees, every muscle in my body had given up all that it held and I submitted to all that one could submit to. I tell you there was no other option, there could never be, maybe there is one who may act otherwise. But to know the heart of one who would act otherwise in such a moment is to know evil in its truest form.

And the light?

It continued, it wasn't a beacon or a lamp or even a light in any normal sense, I am truly sorry that I can't. Can you imagine a rip in all things that allows only hope? I wouldn't blame if you couldn't. The light hadn't been switched on, nor appeared. Who am I to even talk of this? Even if it was I who saw? For I am not I Am. But yes, the light was, and it was blue, and I stood amidst it.

And what did you see?

You have to understand that any definitive question, such as your own, it doesn't work. You want me to describe what was then when we are now. Description of the past is nothing but tyranny, especially this one. And yet I must. In the meadow, the field, grass arching, yes. She stood there first with hands by her sides, clad in blue and white, face pale, eyes downcast, with palms facing out. This is clear to me.

And you just stood?

There is no other option, there couldn't have been, I promise you this.

And then?

And then yes, I stood, as you say. I stood and wept and tried not to blink as the light shone blue over all that was and will be. The figure, in a blink not of my own, was then in prayer. Hands together and the light held and all things flowed and there is a deep sorrow I feel at this that I cannot bring it to you. There was maybe sound of birds, grass in the wind, music, maybe. What matters now? What can I do with this?

And what did you do? What happened?

What did I do? All anyone would ever do is stand there for eternity knowing rest and peace, but such cannot be in this world. And so, in a drift I was back on my bike riding home, everything lodged back somewhere else for me to process later.

Why do you think that was?

I don't know. I only really talk now up to that night and not after it.

Oh?

Would you ever state anything with certainty after such a night?

I don't know.

Me neither.

Something does come to my mind, however...

Yes?

Something you said earlier.

Yes?

You said you weren't happier after that night, that it didn't change anything in that sense?

I did, yes.

Is that because you know you'll never achieve that, as you put it, rest and peace again

No. Those things aren't meant for here.

And so, what is it? Why are you still unhappy?

Because I am an unhappy person.

And you believe that's just how you are?

It is how I am, yes.

So, what of that night?

Without it I wouldn't be, I'm sure of that.

You'd have ended it?

Ended?

Suicide?

Oh, no. It's not that I wouldn't be in that sense. Simply that I wouldn't be who I am now, that night was the present of that point in time and had to be, I both had a say and didn't have a say. Perhaps it is that I never want a say again.

I don't understand.

I wouldn't be, I would have drifted out of existence. Not suicide, that's a material thing, a pragmatic matter of ending the vessel.

Are you thinking about ending your life now?

You're missing the point. But I have no plans, as you would say.

Well, you know how it is with my job.

Practically speaking, I guess I do, yes.

So, are you thinking about it?

I am tired. Do you want the truth for once?

Okay.

One doesn't think of suicide, it's either in your thoughts or it isn't, and if it is in your thoughts, it can only be the foundation. And so, to think about suicide is to think about suicide in all breaks of thought. Unless one is thinking of lunch or dinner one is thinking of suicide.

Practically?

No, no. Thinking about nooses and slit wrists all day would be exhausting, the gaps in thought are filled with the thought of what it would have been to not be. All gaps in thought are filled with the ultimate paradox, what if all that made this possible was never made possible?

I see.

I thought you wanted to know about that night.

I did, but I of course have my concerns.

If I could help you understand you wouldn't, but I can't help you, and so you will.

Well, I think it's time for us to finish up. You up to much this evening?

Just work, as you know.

How is that going?

You know I can't do that kind of chat.

Yes, I do.

What do you really think of that night?

It's not for me to say really. I'm more interested in your analysis of it.

Analysis?

Read, perspective, whatever you like.

But what do you think of it?

Sounds like quite the night. A beautiful night. There's a lot in it, I think.

What?

Best to leave it until next time.

I don't want to go over it again if that's okay.

That's fine. Mind if I ask why?

I wish I could share it, but I can't. I'm sorry.

# Thoughts and Memories of Violet

1:32am, driving 30mph in a 50-zone, an unsurprisingly overweight man half-weeps into his phone which is on speaker mode. He is tired. His skin is clammy and his lower back is sore. The car's aircon smells stale.

...I miss you, Violet. I miss our little Sunday hugs and kisses. I just miss it all.

I couldn't care less Herman. I'm fucking sick of you. I told you not to call me anymore. It's been three nights and you seem unable to just keep to yourself for fuck's sake. Like I said, you can come get your shit on Saturday, I won't be here all day then.

Violet, please. My brother says I need to find a hotel, said I stink up the place. Can we just talk a little?

You do stink up the place. And we did just talk a little.

The phone call ended.

Herman's eyes welled up and his gut gurgled. He caught a glimpse of his phone just as it closed the call. A text from his brother

*you left your gym entry card here but dont bother getting it soon cus karen doesnt want you here. ill mail it once you find somewhere. not like you use it lol*

His brother was right, he didn't use it. In fact, the only reason it had left his wallet was because he was looking for a picture of Violet he'd since tucked away amidst various cards. He must have lost the photograph.

Herman pulled over the car. Some layby in the middle of nowhere, caught between the type of towns where no one amounts to anything. He thinks to himself that he could likely leave his car here indefinitely and no one would care. He enters into a fatigue-fuelled fantasy of living in his car in this layby from now on. The fantasy diverts from optimistic nomadism to realistic urbanism and the image of a decaying fat man melted into his car seat passes through his mind. He imagines the fire service finally discovering his blobby corpse after people living five miles away complain of some dank stench. The emergency services scoop him into a bag, one of them makes a joke about his dead body looking like a gigantic scrotum. With this Herman grabs his phone and with a lot of thick, greasy smears on its screen finds the location of a nearby hotel.

Thanks to technological advances he can see which places have vacancies—or are even open at all —from just scrolling. Other than one bed and breakfast some ten miles away everywhere is full or closed. The place was simply called *The Stay Inn*. He didn't bother looking at anything else, he just needed a bed for the night.

Driving slowly down the backroads on the way to the inn Herman had all but ceased to mentally exist. Enough cognitive action to automatically keep himself within the bounds of the road, but his mind was in truth an indiscernible flurry of memories. Flashes of birthdays and Christmases spent with Violet. When they met. When they first made love. Many which spontaneously arose and he hadn't thought of for many years. Banal moments spent with the woman who was everything to him and had everything of him. His arms were shaking a little and he could feel his lower lip starting to tremble. He bit down on it hard enough for the pain to usurp the sadness. He could taste iron now. His stomach was starting to ache. He had picked up three sausage rolls from a petrol station and eaten them in quick succession before getting the courage to call Violet again. They were lukewarm and didn't taste of much.

Pulling up at a junction. Absolute dead of night, dull-amber lights spewing downwards, eternal coolness, and just nothing around at all. He took a left into a seemingly dilapidated street, though admittedly he could see very little in the darkness and he hadn't bothered to clean his car in years, allowing a crust to build up over the headlights. Everything was vague, coated in a banal and loathsome sepia. His head was clammy and his lower intestine had started to cramp. A pain too close to tummy panic for anyone's liking.

Ahead of him on the left was a crap wooden sign long since left alone, 'THE STAY INN'. A downstairs light was on. He pulled in and grabbed his phone. As he got out his gut gave out a sharp, hot pang and he bent over and clutched it. A little sweaty now. He quick-stepped to the boot and grabbed his rucksack, the same one he'd had since high school, covered in lame band patches and writing from old classmates he hadn't spoken to in years. One piece of the writing said *Herman the fatman*. Slamming the boot and locking the car he all but jogged to the door, hastily slamming against it with his fist. But just as the third and final blow hit against the wood the door creaked open of its own accord. Herman realized then that this was simply an external door leading to a foyer type situation and, being an open and vacant inn, he was meant to just head inside.

Light beady sweat, clammy palms, dank crack, and with a real hot gut, Herman stood in the main lobby of the inn. Before him, just to the left was an unfathomably stereotypical desk setup, complete with an old woman sat behind it with her head in a newspaper.

Excuse me! said Herman with noticeable haste.

Ah, yes. You're here. You're looking for a room, I assume?

Yes, and if you have a toilet I could use-

But if you have found us then there is but one room for you-

Sure, sure, whatever. I just really need that room *right now*!

Do you want to know of *this* room, Sir, and why it is *for you*?

Because I'm paying for it, what? Look, I just need a room right now!

Clutching his gut tightly and attempting to not appear like some helpless loose-gutted infant Herman stared the woman down.

So be it. The key is on the desk. The woman gestured with her head and hand to an old key placed before her.

Thank you, thank you! said Herman practically running over, I'll pop down and give you my details later!

Oh! You won't be coming back later, Sir, the woman said, her head fully returned to the newspaper.

Okay, okay. In the morning then! said Herman, pelting up the stairs.

Farewell, Sir, said the woman. But Herman was out of earshot.

~

Running up to the top of the stairs and looking left and right Herman realized he didn't know the room number. Gut searing deep like some hot iron rod of malice he took a deep breath in. Something called for him to go right. Fuck it, he said and quickly paced rightward down a hall which appeared to go on forever, though Herman was oblivious to this. Passing a few doors, he stopped before Room 28. It felt right. He put in the key. It worked. He quickly went inside and luckily an emergency light allowed him to locate the toilet. Ignoring everything else he slung his rucksack down and, undoing his trousers as he stepped, launched himself toward the loo.

Door ajar, sat in almost darkness with visibility limited to an artificial green, Herman almost doubled-over himself as he let out an acrid torrent of hot shit. He already knew it had gotten onto the upper rim, possibly onto the outside of his cheeks. Good lord, he groaned. Though no man wishes to publicly admit to such, there is no greater relief in this life than making it to a loo in time. In fact, such bowel-based catharsis almost makes the drudgery worth it.

Breathless and aching and empty Herman found himself sat on a cold loo staring into the static-light of his room. He found he could focus on nothing and all edges faded into slight static. He finally sighed with relief and, without pause for any joy, his mind once more prioritized his misery. The thoughts and memories of

Violet returned. He cleaned himself up, pulled on his trousers, and headed into the main room to look for a light-switch.

Flicking on the main light he was greeted by a palpable repetition of all that was normal. As if there existed a single store for all generic hotel and inn furnishings. It was indescribable if for the fact such an act would be, in any descriptive sense, glorifying what was nauseatingly dull. A quiet protruded the room, as if silence itself had ceased for but a moment, if only to allow Herman full assessment of his—admittedly pathetic—situation. Letting out another sigh and feeling the after-effects of his release tighten within him, Herman allowed himself to fall onto the bed. For some time, he simply laid on his back and stared into the ceiling with nothing but the growling of his intestines for company.

He sat up and, finding he had slung his rucksack next to the bed, he reached down and grabbed it. Leaning back against the headboard and drawing the duvet over his legs and lower gut he pulled a four-pack of chocolate bars from his rucksack and began to indiscriminately open and devour them, throwing the wrappers onto the bed and watching them slowly fall to the floor. As he was eating the second bar the act of mastication became trancelike and he stared forward into the in-between and no taste was found. He finished the rest of the bars in much the same state. Feeling full he took his phone from his pocket and slid down, allowing himself to be covered up to his eyes with the duvet, wrapped up and tucked away.

For hours he perused Violet's social media channels. Each photo and video causing a little tug at his congested heart. The main light had turned off by itself but Herman hadn't noticed, his face now solely lit by the glow of images of someone who was not thinking about him. Using what energy he had, he rolled onto his back, holding the phone above his face.

Herman, said a voice from nowhere, quiet, wisp-like. Herman didn't notice, he was captured by a photo of Violet in some swimwear from five years ago. Herman, again a voice from nowhere. Herman looked away from his phone into the darkness and, realizing he obviously wouldn't be able to see anything returned to his phone. Oh Herman! the voice from nowhere was louder now and came from under the bed. Herman dropped his phone onto his face. Fuck's sake, he said.

Herman, you know I'm here. Come see me! the voice curled up from beneath the bed, clearer now. Herman was thinking of the time Violet accidentally fell into the garden pond and this made him come close to weeping and, trying to bite his lip to stifle the tears, he found himself biting the previous wound and in too much pain to continue the stifling, and so, he wept. Little rolling tears falling down his flushed cheeks and onto the bed. Turning over onto his side he pulled one of the pillows deeper under his head and nestled in, staring off into the blackness, only just being able to make out a small wooden table some feet away through his teary eyes.

The room was still and Herman was hot and groggy. None of his memories seemed to stick, being invaded with thoughts of arguments or self-pity. Looking forward, he knew that if he didn't move his eyes then no thought could enter his head, and so that is what he did. Dead-stare straight ahead and stiff as a fat-plank, Herman was a man tucked away, trying to not exist. Oh, come now Herman, you know you wish to see me. The words merely drifted through his consciousness into non-existence, a mindfulness built from misery. Perhaps I should come see you Herman, would you like that? Herman committed to his dead stare. Oh Herman, I'm coming for you..., the voice from beneath him trailing off and surrounding his entire head with a whisper.

~

Wrapped up and pinned in by a musky green duvet. The unrepentant stare ahead. The echo of a belly ache and a covering of light sweat. Herman was there, very much in that spot, his entire existence relied upon him simply being the gargling nothingness he was at that moment within that spot. Head nestled on the edge of the bed breathing up the lightly-dusty air and sighing with every other outbreath. Eyes still set straight ahead as before him slowly arose an emaciated corpse. Into his vision first came the top of the head, wisps of thin greasy hair flew into a non-existent wind. Paper-skin adhered flimsily to an aching skull. Eye sockets hollow but for a trembling infinite black. Nose gone. Teeth protruding and rotten, some sticking through the lips. Grave-risen hellstare into the back of Herman's puppy wet eyeballs. Hey Herman, groaned the corpse from the back of its throat, the lips sliding up and down the rotting elongated tooth stumps. Herman didn't move nor change nor stop his stare. Eyelids heavy and with another small tear he merely allowed a small sigh to fall from his nose. What if he had been more affectionate? He thought, maybe then she wouldn't have told him to leave. The corpse opened its mouth revealing a recursive, non-Euclidean chasm. Maybe I worked too much, he thought. A deep groan from the depths of time itself penetrated the room. Maybe it was my cooking, he thought. The corpse slowly closed its mouth and its eyes became merely empty sockets showing nothing but skull. It remained for some time merely looking through Herman and existing as just a solid corpse. Herman turned over and grabbed his phone again.

He picked up where he'd left off, Violet's social media. The corpse glided slowly and smoothly around the edge of the bed as if on a conveyor belt. Herman intuited it moving around the bed, but as it arrived before him the phone blocked him from seeing it. ...Hey...Herman! the corpse stated a little impatiently. Herman moved the phone down an inch, acknowledging the corpse with nothing more than the same continued stare and then returned to his phone. Don't you want to play, Herman? Herman rolled onto his back and scrolled on his phone for an hour or so, all whilst the corpse continued to verbally prod him. Nothing changed. Herman remained with his memories of Violet. The corpse remained on the floor, upright and empty. Hmmph, Herman complained audibly as his gut once again began to cramp up. Putting his phone in his pocket, he sighed and shifted himself to the front of the bed. He sat on the edge of it and walked the few steps to the loo. Not bothering with finding a light he sat once again on the toilet's held warmth waiting for excremental closure. Once he was comfy, he went to reach for the phone in his pocket and, looking up, noticed from his perch that the corpse had followed him to the loo, sitting itself upright just outside the door he could see now it was nothing more than a torso and head. He looked it up and down and returned to his phone. He tried to call Violet. He noticed it was 4:22am and felt bad, but he still wished she'd picked up, even if to be angry at him, at least he'd get to hear her voice, he thought. What'ya doing Herman? fell from the corpse's open and non-moving mouth. Maybe she's awake and thinking about me? Maybe a call so early in the morning will make her worry? You're so stupid Herman! He thought to himself. You thinking about her Herman? About Violet? Face unchanging, Herman looked over his phone. Oh, you are, aren't you? I can tell.

You can tell? Is that maybe because I'm fucking looking at her social media and calling her? Dumbass.

Oh Herman, you miss her so mu-, at that moment the corpse was interrupted Hnng! Oh, fuck me! another mach 10 jet of half-digested sausage roll echoed off the ceramic, followed by a few remaining straggles of dank, hot sludge. Oof. Wooee. Yeesh. Herman sat back, allowing his stomach to open a bit, feeling the sweet relief of full clearance. He could breathe easy now. Still sat on the toilet, looking up he noticed that the corpse had disappeared, so he returned to his phone and continued scrolling.

~

The room was full of a dread that Herman didn't care about. The wind howled but was drowned out by the sound of Violet's laughter projecting from Herman's phone, a video from a party that happened eight years ago. It was cold but Herman was hot. Some more time passed.

Eventually Herman once again lifted himself from the toilet, cleaned up, and headed back to the bed. Laying down he decided to turn on the bedside lamp. For the first time in a while, he lifted his eyes away from his phone and his thoughts to actually have a look around. He found he couldn't really apprehend the room. The space in-between his eyes and the objects they attempted to perceive appeared as a space with its own agency, vibrating without movement as a vindictive static, through it all colours faded to the opposite of their ideal. To his bewilderment, however, he noticed that the room was but a bed, bathroom, and bedside table. The walls appeared closer than before, the bathroom once a few steps away was now almost touching the duvet overhanging the bed. The window to his left leant over diagonally, towering over him as the geometry of the small table managed to protrude into his peripheral vision. Everything was competing for its sensual sovereignty and yet had little to offer upon arrival. Encased and bereft of essence Herman laid back once more, his head disappearing through the pillows and landing flat against the mattress itself. A horizontal man bellowing vision upward in an attempt for anything at all to descend. Of course, nothing did.

Hello Hermy, said a voice to his right.

Violet? said Herman, and with a weightless turn quickly flicked onto his side.

Yes, yes, it's me, said the thing staring back at him. All covered with the images and veils and thoughts and memories and offerings of something that pretended with all its energy to be that person it most certainly was not. But Herman expended everything to believe. Just for a moment.

Oh Violet, when did you get here? It doesn't matter...I'm so sorry...you need to listen...I-I just, well, I dunno, where do I start-

That which was not Violet looked back at him and through him, fake eyes glazed over with nihil. Every contour and dimple empirically correct, but that which was beneath shone through black with its wrongness.

I think I've been so silly and I just don't what to do or say and I don't know what you want. But, yes, I'm so sorry for it all, I don't know what, but I'm sorry for it all and I want to come home. The thing too heavy now and sunk further down than was right. Then it licked its lips and the tongue had too much saliva and it drooled off the end and disappeared into the air.

Oh, Violet please I beg of you, I beg I beg, oh please, when did you get here and I-I just miss you, oh please-

The thing let out an almost indiscernible croak.

-what? Oh, tell me tell me, please Violet. Let me try get myself together. Sorry for all this, it's just, I really miss you. I'm sorry for the calls, I'm sorry for bothering you, just, if...if we could just talk, you know? I think that would do us good and we can sort this all out.

All the while Herman spoke the croak was gaining volume and now held itself as a monotonous dry creek edging into the static.

I cannot understand you dear Violet? Please, I think we just need to talk, I think it would be really good, you know?

The creak only got louder. Rusted throat scratching loud into the dark, erasing anything that came close.

Violet, please, I cannot hear anything.

The creak turned into a screech then a scream, raised to such malicious heights that it vibrated Herman's eardrums. His teeth hurt. His eyes pulsed. Then it stopped and there was a silence worse than all noise.

...Violet? Herman said, staring at the thing as its tongue protruded once more covered in a thin milky slime. A tongue too long was left hanging. Herman gazed at the corner of its mouth and it wasn't right, it sat against all law, a dimple vectored into impossibility. And he stared and more time passed and over such time the shape of the thing contorted itself into angles of delirium. Legs that pulled the feet into the shins as the knees rose and bent upon themselves, torso collapsing as a little fan, head remaining and neck extended to hold it in place. In an instant the skin crumples into a dry wrapper, the failed torso and legs drop through the bed. The head remains for a few seconds attached to a neck seeking to drag it down, mouth pooling inward and eye-sockets bulging, a final Heeeh! as the thing drops into non-existence.

Cya Violet. Sometimes things are like this I guess, Herman said.

Herman checked his phone. It was 3:12am. He had been lying next to that which was not Violet for almost an entire day. How beautiful, he thought.

~

His phone battery was at 9%. He checked his rucksack and found he must have left his charger in the car. He placed his phone down and looked around. The main light was now on and the room stretched for miles in every direction. The bathroom somehow always where it should be, the bedside table too, but the walls had exited their definition. Sitting on the edge of the bed Herman looked out into an endless expanse lit beige. He stood up and started walking forward for no real reason at all. He passed where the window once was and felt he should be falling to the street below but he didn't. He kept walking. He kept thinking about Violet.

He looked back and saw the bed was but a dot on the horizon. Hands in his pockets he turned his back to everything and allowed himself to embrace the boring abyss. It didn't overcome him nor infect him; it didn't wash over him nor cause him insanity. The beige-abyss reflected back the inanity of it all. If only Violet was here, he said. Thinking of little if anything at all.

He had been there some time. Walking this direction and that in this place where all directions are none. At some point or other he decided to turn back, perhaps get some sleep, he thought. As he stepped in the reverse direction to his left a clump of thin spindled lines emerged from afar. As he locked his gaze the mesh of hair-thin black lines shot before him. A little group of people made only from black lines, stringed beings attempting to hold themselves together. Not scrawny flesh but pure geometric lines containing being, faces trying to carve out any border, yearning for depth. This small group of palpitating string people looked up and down at Herman. They made noises not heard before.

Some collapsed and others stretched as elastic thread to points on the eternal horizon, an uncontrollable panic of form. Thoughts and emotion uncontained and purged to become points of panicked hell. One of the string people formed a face on the floor alike a child's stick-figure drawing. It frowned up at Herman before the mouth opened and let out dead air. Sound jutting in and out of existence, screams and shrieks, single tones and caustic harshness, a fit of non-rhythm abound as the string-people panicked and promoted only seizure. Herman looked through them all and found himself caught in a memory long since thought forgotten. Violet enjoyed knitting, he said. A final searing digital beep that left Herman's ears ringing and the string people were gone.

As he turned around, he found himself before his bed and so he got on and laid down. Closing his eyes, taking a breath, opening them, the room was normal again, but it didn't matter, he thought. He looked down toward the end of the bed and noticed that the bathroom door was closed. Yet, as he continued to stare forwards it began to slowly open. It stopped moving halfway. From behind it in the half-light emerged the face of a decaying clown whose skin was more makeup than flesh. It let out the sound of a horn and tried to emerge further. Forget it, Herman said, and turned over, grabbing his phone and noticing it still had 3% battery. He decided to try scroll back to the first ever messages he had sent to Violet. As he neared messages sent just over three years ago the phone went black and he could see both his reflection and his thick greasy thumbprints on the glass. Maybe if I'd lost weight, he thought to himself.

At times he thought there were people outside, people watching him, voices that desired and owned things he never knew were within him. But his eyes were a gloss and he would pick up the phone out of habit, an attempt to see but a single image of Violet, before letting it fall away after once again realizing it was out of battery. Eventually the birds started tweeting and the light reluctantly entered.

~

In the morning, he found himself rising early with an odd clarity of thought, as if everything was settled. Nothing more dangerous than settling all matters than by simply declaring them meaningless. He grabbed his things and left the room. As he walked down the stairs he was greeted by the old woman once again.

Sir, it has been quite some time I believe, and you are the first to ever-

I would like to check-out, interjected Herman, how much do I owe you?

Owe?

For the room. What's your rate, I never asked?

Oh sir, that is not what-

Herman proceeded to take out a wad of mottled cash from his rucksack.

Here. That's all I have on me. That should cover it. Thanks for the room.

But sir, the room-

Was fine. Bye.

And with that he left the *The Stay Inn*. Finding himself sat outside in his car plugging the phone immediately into the charger and waiting for it to load up. He looked up and saw the old woman looking down at him with a perplexed stare. He gave her a slight nod.

~

He drove around for a while after this until he eventually returned to the layby where he had fantasized about living.

Two days later a police car pulled in behind Herman's car because of a complaint from an anonymous dog-walker. The policeman exited his vehicle and walked over to Herman's car.

We're going to need to get some people over to my location, the policeman said over the radio, looks like some fat sack of shit has killed himself.

# The Shed

The young boy was stood in his grandparent's kitchen.

The large kitchen window looked out onto a boxed-in garden.

At the end of the garden, over to the right, was a shed. This is what the young boy looked at.

Some evenings his grandad would go down there and the young boy would see the dim light coming from the shed window. His grandma would be quick to say Oh, he's out there tinkering again.

Come on, let's get some biscuits! and usher him off for biscuits, but he never ate any of the biscuits and just went up to bed.

One day when grandad and grandma were in the lounge the young boy snuck past the lounge door and stood in the kitchen.

He stood at the window and just looked at the shed. It was a very basic single door shed with no windows. The wood was very dry and it was neat, symmetrical.

The garden was always quiet and the young boy didn't like to play in it.

One weekend grandma was very ill, very sick. Grandad was looking after her upstairs in their bedroom and he asked the young boy to get her a glass of water. Grab us a glass of water chap, will ya?

The young boy went downstairs and grabbed a glass of water at the kitchen sink. Before going back upstairs he glanced out at the shed and made a decision.

There's the water grandad, I'm going to watch TV.

Okay, keep it down though.

Okay. Is grandma going to be okay?

She'll be fine, you go watch TV.

The young boy went downstairs, into the lounge, turned on the TV, and then left the lounge and stood in the kitchen, once again staring out of the window at the shed. He got his face real close to the window.

He checked the hallway to see if anyone was there. No one. He went back into the kitchen and opened the back door, stepped out into the garden, and closed the door behind him as quietly as he could.

He walked very fast to the end of the garden, the shed appearing before him hastily, almost startling him. He looked down at the grass and saw it to be oddly even. Many of the blades stood perfectly upright.

The shed seemed to impose on him. The young boy undid the latch and pulled open the door. He smelt nothing. An empty gust of air that left a subtle ringing in his ears. He stepped inside and closed the door behind him, checking back at the kitchen to see if anyone had come down. They had not.

Inside the shed was a small worktop that ran along the left side. There was nothing on it. A small cupboard at the far end. He checked inside. There was nothing in it. He looked over the inside of the shed again. In the top right-hand corner, at the end, a small box, attached to the shed itself. It appeared to have a small piece of rope attached so one could pull down the front.

The young boy jumped and missed. Jumped and missed. Jumped and missed. Jumped and grabbed and ripped the box to the floor. Bits of wood everywhere. A light crash. Dust. Something else. Something else still by chance tucked under one of the broken bits of wood. The young boy reached down and removed the piece of wood.

He held what looked like a small, contortioned piece of black metal. Bulbous, rounded, and without a single place of reflection. It felt to him as if it was trying to stretch itself out, trying to break itself, trying to push out from the inside of its own matter like a self-conscious bundle of ligaments. He held it as it yearned and creaked in his mind. There was pain here and he felt it all. There was terror here and it bellowed into his being. The screams ran cacophonous in his ears. His left eardrum trembled and released a slight mucous. Sweat ran as he felt their demise. The young boy's eyes full of tears as his lips could not manifest the form to quiver. Held in place and colder than possible, blue skin grinning into its own self-built death. The wailing filled his stomach, his muscles; his body the bawling of terror itself. Eyes rolled into the back of skull and corneas searing into cerebellum, the weep protruded from the back of his throat and fell as a whimper, a little squeak of something disappearing. Legs stiff, back curving forward, mouth agape and pleading, pleading.

And yet he sank deeper than anyone before and he saw it all and the heavens ask for forgiveness for such sights. Falling to the floor a cripple of existence he had seen that which cannot be taken back and life in all its black glory can never be the same again. Have you ever felt the rupture in all things that the sane try to keep at bay but shall overflow into the blood of all the white lambs? The parasite came forth and took all once again, only to re-enter into its own suffering. Pain begets pain begets pain, the only error in the cosmos founded within this negentropic fount of black water, flowing now, and forever, into life's eternal child.

~

It was about ten years until the young boy went to see his grandparents again. By this time, he was a young man and they were even older, both entering that stage of life where even too strong of a breeze might kill them.

His grandad answered the door. Long time, he said.

Yeah, the young man said.

Want to come in?

Sure.

Tea?

Okay.

They stood in the kitchen and the young man looked at the floor. Then at the worktop. Then at his grandad. Then the kettle. Then he looked at the window itself. Then he looked out toward the shed, trying not to focus, letting his vision go through it. It was the same as it had been that day. His grandad didn't bother finishing the teas.

What do you remember?

Not a lot. Remember waking up in the spare room at some point. When did you find me?

Maybe 30 minutes after you told us you were going to watch TV.

Ah. So, you remember then?

I remember it exactly. I'm glad your grandma was sick and didn't see you like that.

Yeah.

She knew, though.

...oh.

White and blue you were. Pulsing. I could hear your bones snapping but you were perfectly straight.

They stood for a long while in silence. Eventually the grandma came down from upstairs.

Oh, hello, he didn't come tell me you'd arrived.

Haven't been here too long.

Oh, okay.

They looked at each other, all three of them, and something had been undone.

Well, I'll be in the lounge.

Okay. Good to see you grandma.

You too.

She walked off.

Come on, the grandad said, opening the back door and heading down the garden to the shed. The young man followed. They both entered the shed and it was the same as it had been on that day. The little box that held the error had been repaired.

Did you repair it?

No.

Then wh-

Don't know.

What is it?

Don't know.

When did it-

I don't know anything about it.

But you also-

Yeah. I've seen.

Does it ever...decrease?

No.

What do you figure it is, generally, abstractly?

Knowledge of a different kind. Knowledge we can't know.

And at night?

It doesn't stop and you can't be released. There's no reward here or there, and no end.

# Bone Feet Don't Have Hair

Look, the Dr knows about it already, so if I could just-

Sir, I know the Dr knows about it because I can see your records, and it says here the Dr has given you advice on what to do.

Yes, but it's getting worse.

It's getting worse?

Yes, it's getting worse quite rapidly.

Rapidly?

Yes, on the walk in this morning a finger fell off-

Sir, if you're going to waste our time, I'm going to have to ask you to leave and I could also take you off our patient register.

I'm deadly serious.

Deadly?

Yes, a finger fell off, I have it here with me in my pocket.

Sir, if you've been asked to hand in a sample you need to bring it in one of the supplied containers and place it in the basket over there, I don't, we don't directly handle samples.

But it's my finger, it fell off and I have it-

Sir! I'm asking you to not waste our time. If you would like to book an appointment with Dr Gate then you are welcome to.

But...okay, well, can I book an emergency appointment?

Is it an emergency?

Well, my finger-

I know about your finger, as I said, all samples have to be placed in the container, and only if you've been asked to provide one by the Dr.

It is an emergency!

Sir, don't raise your voice at me. Are you struggling for breath?

No, it's just that-

Sir. Do you have any profuse bleeding?

Profuse?

Yes, profuse.

What's profuse?

The bleeding.

No, what does it mean?

I'm not sure, I think it means a lot. Sir, if you're going to waste my time-

I'm not I just don't know what profuse-

Sir, please don't interrupt my questions, I am just trying to help. Do you have any...serious bleeding?

No.

Any problems with urine or your stool?

My finger has literally fallen off and I have it in my pocket!

Sir! I'm going to put the phone down now!

But-

Sir! There are people on the line waiting.

And so, the phone call ended

~

It had begun the Tuesday before, well, the Monday night, in fact. See, he, the rotting man, had felt pressure above one of his upper molars. Not pain, pressure. He tried to think little of it, but being the hypochondriac that he is, continued to research the symptoms online until roughly four in the morning, at which point, he yawned wide and the tooth in question fired out of his mouth onto the keyboard, digitally printing the letter Y in the URL bar. The tooth flew out with such speed that after hitting the keyboard it bounced off the screen and was nowhere to be seen. The rotting man, with his mouth suspiciously dry, could not find the tooth, even after some two hours of searching. He stopped, around 6am, not because he wanted to, but because he felt horrifically nauseous at the thought of his head being filled with pressure.

He figured it was useless going to sleep and so sat on the sofa with a cloth in his mouth, even though there was no bleeding and, whilst in a place of dizziness, watched early morning TV. Early morning TV may as well not exist. Sometimes it's reruns of older shows, cheap, I guess for the networks to run. But they don't fit. Shows about people from other countries doing things that people from other countries do, people going into bars and having evening meals broadcast at 6am, truly grotesque, awful, even. He felt himself watching the TV and shed a tear or two, there was no emotion, just the tears that ran also into the cloth.

It came time to ring the doctor's office. 8am the lines opened. He called on the dot. The automated voice on the other side told him he was fourth in the queue and he waited some 20 minutes before he spoke to anyone. He told them of the tooth and the pressure and, in turn, they told him to go to the dentist. He told them he didn't think this was a dental matter and, in turn, they told him it was because it concerned a tooth. He was tired though, very tired in fact. In fact, and it was truly a fact, he wasn't just tired because he had been up all night, he was tired just because he was tired. He couldn't remember a time he hadn't been tired and, in words of his own, he told himself this fact a few times. And so, after the phone call, which he considered a nothing, a nothing in a long line of nothings past, present, and future, he decided to take a nap.

As he did so, the man, very tired indeed, leant on his hand, and it was at that point that the aforementioned finger in question just fell off, Oh it's popped off, he said to himself. And it was that popping off of the finger that led to the aforementioned phone call concerning the aforementioned finger, a phone call that was dialled mere minutes after the last, but, due to waiting and music and all kinds of imagined nonsense going on at the other end, wasn't answered until an hour later, at which point the aforementioned phone call regarding the aforementioned tooth felt like a distant memory. And when he, the man, finally did finish the second phone call, which, as we have seen came to no conclusion, he decided to retreat back to the nap he had already decided upon before even making the phone call concerning the aforementioned finger.

He awoke sometime after three. Awaking amidst the revenge of a nap. His body treated the sleep as a long nap and adults aren't supposed to nap. Adults are punished for it, harshly. Disorientation, dehydration, dishevelment, and disorder. One awakes to such a chaotic situation that one could be shot point blank and only mumble something about dinner. Sickening, he thought. The most disgusting thing was how his body felt. All grim like it was covered in a thin layer of grime or grease or saliva or bile. If he didn't shower, he thought, surely he would just lie down as some terminally ill patient of the earth and slowly die in his sheets.

He pulled off his clothes as he walked to the shower, leaving his socks for last. As he pulled the right sock off, half-losing his balance, all his toenails flew off, some of them hitting the wall and leaving thin red streaks on the paint. Oh dear, he said to himself as he sighed. Placing his foot down in a strange hot delight, he pulled the other off slowly to find not only were his nails gone, but all the skin from his foot. Bloody hell, a bone foot, he said. He placed it down on the floor and felt nothing. As he walked to the shower his right foot ached and his bone foot clunked. Still, true enough to the needs of a man who really did stink, he got in the shower. The water hit him with a palpable lukewarmness that was worse than if it were cold. He sighed and, as he did so for the second time, right after the first, his hair began to run down his body. Seriously? he half-yelled. And, still, he washed and wished to be clean. As the shower neared its end he wondered and questioned and eventually gave in, bringing his bone foot upward to take a look. All the skin was all sealed off already. He prodded and poked and it felt all puffy. He soaped up his bone foot and gave it a rinse.

~

Hello?

Yes, hello?

Sorry, is that the doctors?

Yes...how can we help?

Sorry, it's just that I'm not sure if you could hear me.

I can hear you.

You can hear me now?

Yes, sir. How can I help?

Is there a delay?

I don't think so.

I guess we wouldn't know.

How can I help?

I need to book an appointment please.

Okay, what's it concerning?

I'm not sure how to explain it really.

If it's a personal matter sir, know that everything you say is confidential, we just need to know where is the best place to direct you.

A personal matter?

Yes?

Isn't all doctors stuff personal?

Well, yes, but okay, very personal stuff, is it like that?

Like what?

Like your penis or testicles-

Oh, no-

-or anus, or stool-

Oh, no, it's my feet and hair.

The hair on your feet?

No. My feet, separately. And then my hair, that was after.

Okay, what was after? Sorry, what has happened, what do you need help with?

Okay. The-

Okay?

Sorry I was about to tell you.

Oh, okay, go on.

Okay. Is there a delay?

I don't think so. Please, go on.

Okay so-

Okay.

...

Go on.

Me toenails...my toenails have gone off my foot. On my left foot my toenails have gone.

Where have they gone?

What do you mean?

Your toenails have gone?

Yeah, when I took my sock off, they flew off.

Is it painful?

It aches a bit.

Is there bleeding?

Not majorly.

So just that your toenails have *gone off*?

Well, yeah, but on the other foot-

So, both feet?

Well, no. On the left the toenails have...gone off, and on the right most of the whole foot is gone. I've got a bone foot.

You've got bone foot? Or you've got *a* bone foot?

Is it a thing? I dunno, I guess I got bone foot?

Okay, we can get you in this evening if you're free?

That would work. What time?

In roughly two hours. It would be a sit-and-wait appointment.

Okay that works, but what about my hair?

Bone feet don't have hair, see you soon sir.

~

And, so, he went to the Dr and as he sat in the waiting room with his smooth head and with his bone foot covered by a sock, he thought about his body, and how, oddly, he'd never really cared much about his toenails and, in all honesty, won't miss them all that much. He started to mentally list body parts he felt he wouldn't really miss if they disappeared. His list contained only two additional things, the small boney bump on each wrist and his nipples. He whispered I wouldn't miss my nipples to himself in the waiting room and a woman clutched her yellow-skinned child close to her chest. He understood that what he said was odd and he didn't mean to say it out loud, he felt like audibly trying to rectify the situation, but went through a good five-minute fantasy and concluded it was for the best to remain quiet. By the time he had finished imagining his conversation with the woman in the waiting room—which concluded with her falling in love with him, of course—he was called into the doctor's office.

As he stood his bone foot gave way and he stumbled onto the chairs across from him. The Dr tutted and the woman clutched her child so tight it puked a load of sputum down itself, Oh God, she said. The rotting man said sorry. The woman said it's fine.

The child said I've got yawn dees. The woman said it's called jaundice. The man said that doesn't sound good. The Dr said I'm waiting. The main said But, me bone foot. The doctor said I'll be in my office and walked off. He limped and got there without any help; such is how most things are.

~

What seems to be the problem?

Well-

Okay, I can see here that Katie-

Katie?

That's our secretary.

Oh, okay, I spoke to-

You have lost all the hair on your foot, is that right?

No. I lost my hair and I lost-

You've lost your hair?

Yes.

On your head?

Yes.

Could I see?

Well, I'm not wearing a hat... Even so, that isn't the main thing?

Okay, well, we will start with the hair.

Well, as you can see, I've got no hair.

Didn't you used to have a shaved head?

I haven't been to the Dr in-

3 years and 8 months.

I guess.

Well, not you guess, it's right here, on the computer.

But even so, I've never had a shaved head.

I'm sure you did.

No. Even so-

Even so.

Sorry?

Your hair?

It's gone. Look, not even follicles.

Any pain?

No. It just fell out in the shower.

A new shampoo?

I hadn't even put on any shampoo.

So, you don't use shampoo? It could be that. Though, it's likely a different water heaviness.

Heaviness?

Hardness, is that it?

The water is hard around here.

Yeah. And the hair has also fallen from your feet?

Could I show you my feet?

Would you like me to look at your feet?

Yes.

Yes?

Yes...please?

Do you think it's needed?

I think so.

Hmm, okay, lay down on the bed please.

So, the left foot has-

I'll take a look, often self-diagnosis causes a lot of psychosomatic problems.

Okay.

Okay. So, with your right foot it seems there's no problems that I can see. Any pain?

My toenails are gone.

Did you have toenails before now?

Yes.

Last time you were here you had toenails?

Yes.

All of them, on this foot?

Yes.

Okay, well, is there any pain?

No.

Well, I can't say I'm worried.

Oh.

Try not to focus on it for now, let's look at the other and go from there.

Okay.

Okay, so here I'd say that this is mostly down to the bone, it's around 70% a foot of bone.

The woman-

Katie?

Yeah, she said it could be bone foot?

Bone foot or *a* bone foot?

I don't know the difference.

Too much searching online.

Is it bad?

Does it hurt?

Not at all.

And you can walk on it.

Mostly, I tripped in the waiting room.

You likely got up too fast.

My foot is mostly bone, though.

Right now I wouldn't know what to suggest. If it gets worse, give us a call. I see on your record that you suffer from major depressive disorder, how are things?

Under control yes.

Have you tried CBT?

I'll give you a ring if anything changes.

And so the rotting man left the premises.

~

He arrived home from the doctors around 9am and had the whole day ahead of him. He had nothing planned and this, for him, meant that nothing would be planned. The trip to the doctors was the event of the day and now that was done with the rest of the day was handed over to fate. He sat on the sofa and enacted a bodily act of exhaustion before now he had only seen as ridiculous, that is, he slumped back hard, sighed deeply, and brushed his hands roughly over his face and scalp many times. With this his scalp fell off. It slid off like a thin pancake of putty giving up its owner, falling with a slight slap behind the sofa. The rotting man shot up with a jolt, half-looked behind him, and, with a deep, deep sigh, fell back into the sofa.

He had ridden his bike to and from the doctors. As he sat on the sofa he thought of his feet, his toenails, his hair, his scalp, and as he did, he leant forward and pulled up his trousers and found that both feet were now bone feet, the socks slid off at some point of their own accord. He stared beyond the feet to see his bare ankles and the bottom of both shins, neatly wrapped with flesh like singular racks of lamb. He wasn't sure what to do and likewise was unsure as what not to do. The day was too open. Please, he said, give me *something*.

Getting on for midday he finally picked himself up from the sofa, losing his lower back fat as he did so, it fell from under his shirt with a dry splat. Just as he went to walk over to the kitchen, to fix himself some raw carrot and hummus, the phone rang. Hello.

Hello.

Mum?

I was just ringing to see how you were, if you're busy I can-

No, it's fine, just unwell.

Unwell? How? Not anything I can catch, I hope?

You can't catch anything from a phone call.

Other than sarcasm! What is it? You tired again?

I'm rotting.

Aren't we all.

What?

Anyway, I was ringing to tell you that Steph, you know, next door, to the right, well she is going to the council about the border between her house and mine and-

I thought you were ringing to see how I was?

Yes, and you said you were fine.

I said I was rotting.

Okay, well, she's going ahead with it and that will mean that you need to move your stuff from the garage.

But the garage-

Oh, don't argue. Do I need it?

Alright, well I can't get over that soon really, as I say I'm unwell.

Well, if you could get over tomorrow or the day after, it'll need to be moved.

Alright.

Okay. Anyway, you okay, everything all good over there?

I said earlier.

Okay, that's good to hear.

Yeah.

Yeah.

Yeah.

Anyway, always good to hear from you, thanks for ringing.

Okay, bye.

Bye. See you in a day or two to get your stuff. Okay.

Sure.

Okay, bye.

Bye. Bye now.

Bye.

Bye, bye then.

Bye.

The rotting man went to put the phone back in its holster and lost a hand in the process. Clasped to the phone, the heavy hand fell to the floor with a dull, boring thud. Hello? Hello? You still there?

Mum, the phone's fallen.

Why has it fallen? I hope this isn't charging me.

I'll sort it. Bye.

Bye.

The man picked up the phone by clasping his rotten hand with his other hand. This better not be charging me.

It isn't. Why don't you put down your phone?

Don't talk back. What's wrong with yours anyway?

Bye.

With that the man placed his dismembered hand that held the phone onto the holster and listened for the click. He sighed once more. Just as he'd finished the phone rang, also, once more. He, again, picked up his hand with his other hand that still held the phone. Hello?

Hello?

Mum?

Yes?

You just rang?

But you put the phone down?

It fell.

Okay.

Okay.

Bye then.

I'll have to look at my bill, I guess.

Okay, bye mum.

Yes, bye this time.

Bye.

He pushed his hand into the top of his other hand into the phone and heard, again, a clear click, and, with another sigh, went to get his meal. Using his remaining hand, he prepared a plate of carrots and hummus. Grabbing the small plate of nice raw, crisp carrots and nice fresh hummus he, the rotting man, once again sat on the sofa, feeling oddly content as some of that light from the sun fell into the room.

He took a carrot and loaded the end with hummus. He took a big bite and the teeth it pushed with themselves pushed deep into his gums. The hummus fell onto his tongue and he took the carrot back out of his mouth and reloaded it with hummus. Trying again on the other side he found those teeth too were pushed into his gums. Once more he brought the carrot out, dipped, and tried to use his front teeth, like a little bunny boy, but they merely bent against the carrot and then fell and tumbled down his throat. He coughed a little and said to himself that They're gone forever. He dipped his new arm nub into the hummus and licked it off. After he had eaten what he could, he thought, once more, of ringing the Dr, but felt only that it would be a pointless endeavour. This will pass too he said to himself, thinking that didn't sound quite right.

He walked himself off to his bedroom, his left arm falling off in the process, along with his lower lip, left ear, and the back of his neck. He got to his bedroom and fell back onto his bed with a sigh that seemed to knock all the wind out of him. A hard cough and his two front teeth shot out so fast they lodged themselves into the ceiling plaster. He sighed and spit flew all over his face.

He awoke to the sight of his left leg. It had rolled off during the night, falling in such a way to be leaning against the bed post like a false leg made of real flesh. He, the rotting man, went to wipe his eyes and forgot about the reality of his new nub and simply butted his forehead. He used his other hand to try push the sleep from his eyes and dislodged his left eyeball, pushing it upwards into his forehead. As he pulled his hand away, he noticed the two fingers he had used were bent back all floppy. Floppy fingers he said to himself. He thought now that he had best call the doctors again, yet in truth, his heart dropped at such an idea for he did not want to pester them, there is nothing worse he thought, than being a nuisance, getting in the way, wasting time. With these thoughts he found himself feel angry and sad, thinking back to a childhood that he could only describe as a disappointment. Not a Christmas where you didn't get what you wanted, but one where you did and felt all the worse for it. Isn't that life? he thought to himself unable to wipe the tears from his remaining eye.

Pushing himself from his bed with his remaining arm, the rotting man, fully nude, guided himself along the wall to the phone, hopping as he did. He found that where he touched the skin it fell from him as if it had its own life and he a burden of the most basic kind. Little bone foot tapping as he hopped to the phone. With the final, further hop to the phone he landed with a slam that caused the skin of his nose to slide off.

Hello?

Hello, is that the doctors?

Yes?

Is there a delay?

I don't think so.

I need to book an appointment.

What's the problem?

I am rotting.

You're rotting?

Yes, I'm all falling apart.

Right...sir, listen, you have called before and if I remember right, you wasted our time then.

No, look, I am serious, I am to pieces, I am pieces, I am rotting.

Sir. I am going to have to ask you to not call again. Bye.

Bye.

~

Hello. Mum?

Yes, hello. What do you need?

Could you possibly give me a lift to the doctors?

What happened to your bike?

I'm too unwell-

Well, I'm not taking you if it's something I can catch.

You can't, I just really need you to take me.

Do you have an appointment?

Not yet, but I think they will give me one.

Well, I'm not waiting around.

I'll wait all day and then give you a call.

So, I just have to sit by the phone all day?

No, I, look I just really need a lift.

Right. Okay, when?

Can you come pick me up now?

Now?

Yeah, now?

Right now?

I really need to go.

Right okay whatever. Let me get my stuff I'll be there soon.

When?

I don't know I have to get ready first, it's early.

Okay, call me when you're outside.

Okay, see you then.

Thank you.

Sure. Bye.

Bye.

~

As he stepped away from the phone his remaining leg gave way and shot out from under him and the rest of him plummeted to the ground with a thud. He pulled himself by his remaining arm to the front door and then to the end of the hallway and then down the two flights of stairs and then pushed himself up and opened the front door and then dragged himself onto the front step and laid cheek against slab looking out at the road, a naturally sewn up limbless rotten husk of forgotten shit waiting for his diagnosis. His mother pulled up some time later and said Oh for goodness' sake get over yourself as he dragged himself to the car door. Get in the back she said, and so he did, lying across the seats. If I get pulled over, you're paying the fine. They arrived and she told him that she was Going into town to get some bits and bobs, I'll be back later. He pulled himself out and she drove off.

There he was, the rotting man, dragging himself by one arm across the doctor's carpark and into the foyer. His chin scraped and lost all its flesh, his remaining eye caught a gust of wind and sunk into his skull, his ears were long since forgotten, and his entire chest had sunken deep. His remaining pull left him flat on his front on the foyer carpet, perhaps some three feet beyond the automatic doors. Blind, deaf, breathless, and tired, the rotting man rested on his boney nose face down. A few people walked past him both ways and one young boy looked at him and said Mum, that man's all gone! Katie from the desk walked over and asked what time his appointment was but by then the rotting man's voice box has dissipated into a pulp and had been wretched up onto the carpet. She told him if it's that bad, he'd have to wait in the secluded section. He didn't move. I'll get the Dr, she said. His remaining arm rolled away and fell to bits, he crapped up inside himself and let out a gargle gasp apology, his swansong. The Dr arrived and said You should have come sooner.

# The Place That's Green, Like Seafoam

He held the old video tape in his hand, down by his side, and looked at his wife all tired and glum. She was a thin woman who almost always wore a blue flowery dress. He was average build and held a paunch that, just then, seemed to hide the tape. The tape, the tape, the tape, she said, getting more exasperated as she stared into the sink's half-murky water. Why must you always...always-, she'd lost all the words, -...*look into* things! The ceramics clattered and the watered spattered onto her blueness. Remember what my father used to say, *if in doubt, back away*.

He didn't say that at all and you know it, he used to say *if in doubt, check it out*!

Well, he was an old fool then! Just get rid of the bloody thing.

~

But he couldn't, of course, get rid of it. How could one? It's what it is to be human, to investigate things, even an overturned box on the sidewalk is an event. It doesn't matter how many times man is disappointed by what he finds, he will ever go on searching beneath the overturned and tucked away simply because it's overturned and tucked away. And, also, of course, he had found it in the attic of their—lovely and nice—holiday property. It was in a light green cloth bag, inside a black sack, inside a wooden box, itself wrapped tight with tape and affixed to the back of one of the far support beams with masses of cord. He rarely went up there. Perhaps this was the fourth or fifth time he had done so, he had thought to himself, and never once had he stepped to the end. Nothing called him but a practical leak, one which his wife said she wasn't bothered by and asked that he not go in the attic, but he did, and he stepped to the end, and turned back, and in the dim light saw the strange rectangle of cord and tape bound and bound again to the beam. He stood for a while just looking at it, all that dried cord and half-peeling tape, strange.

He moved with an odd clarity and purpose back to the attic hatch, down the ladder, down the stairs, through the kitchen, past his wife, out of the front door, to the car, opening the boot, grabbing his toolbox, and then back, following his steps with an automaticity arising from nowhere, like the hue of a wind coming and going again. His wife even said don't don't don't under her breath, but he had passed and passed again, and each time she made the sign of the Cross all meek and humble like, but it didn't even graze him. He went back up and banged his shoulder on the hatch, but he didn't really notice, and then he was back at the beam, legs splayed across the roof beams, leaning down like the arch of Nuit to balance his toolbox on the rightmost joist. Opening it all carefully, believing that if it or he fell they would crash through the ceiling, maybe to land in front of a wife all weeping, or maybe just a general fall.

He took a hunting knife out from his toolbox and went to saw the top most cord, but as he pushed against all that was bound the knife dragged straight down and the dry cords pinged away with a snap of horrid dust. The box remained covered and held by tape, a cracking black cube before him. He placed the knife back in the toolbox, held to the black object and tugged. It came away with ease. Some of the tape being pulled to pieces, little blacks fragments floating away. He held it in his hands like an idol, stepped back across the beams and perched himself like a big old crow just in front of the hatch, where there were loose boards and loose light. He grabbed the tape and pulled it away. It all came off with ease, not a speck was left, and the box appeared pristine. A varnished box, walnut maybe. He lifted the latch to find the black waves of burlap. He fumbled with the black to reveal a light green cloth, which he unfolded to reveal what appeared to be papers and the videotape. Checking the box over he found nothing more. Checking the sack over he found nothing more. He placed them down and, with the light green wrap in his hand he turned out the light, descended, closed the hatch, and went downstairs.

He had sat in the kitchen, placing the package on the table. She had her back to him as she falsely wiped the worktop. He looked over the papers, skimming them, finding them to hold no concurrent thread. Some were whole, some were clippings, some old, some very old. He noticed that one dated back to the 1800s and thought maybe this was an antique collection of sorts. He held the tape and looked at its label. I BEG OF YOU TO HELP ME it said in clear black letters. Well, what is it then? his wife finally questioned, stopping her wiping as she did so.

Oh, just some papers and an old video tape.

What are the papers?

Antiques, I think.

Oh. And the tape?

I'm not sure, it says-

Well, I guess it doesn't matter so much then. A load of old rubbish, chuck it all away, it doesn't half smell.

I can't really smell anything.

Because you had that sinus thing-

No, I mean, I can smell, but I can't smell this stuff. Doesn't smell of anything. Nothing at all. Smells clear.

Smells clear? What a weird thing to say. Right, well, if you're going to be playing around with that *crap* then I'm going to read my book.

Okay, well, I have a few bits to do outside anyway.

~

That afternoon he found himself getting into his car and driving into the local town. He told himself and told his wife that he was going to buy a few bits for dinner, but he found himself aimlessly wandering around, looking in charity shops and shop windows. Before long, on the outskirts of town, he discovered that he was in a second-hand store filled with bric-à-brac and objects that can never be entirely dusted. Before long he held under his arm a VHS player and an assortment of cables. An old man reading a book in a wing back chair half-shouted Two pounds! Put it in the tray. And so, he looked before him and saw an old desk with a metal tray on top that looked as if it had been removed from a dentist's office. It held a few notes and coins. He dropped in a five-pound note and left.

As he arrived home, he noticed his wife, in a different blue dress, standing inside and looking out of the window at his arrival, tucking the net curtains behind her. He sat in the car for a minute or so as they stared at each other. She looked at him as if she had made the greatest mistake in even knowing of his existence, he thought only of the strange welling up inside him, a giddiness that felt anarchic in nature. He grabbed the VHS player and got out of the car with his eyes set on her, though truthfully looking through her. She glanced once down at the VHS player under his arm and walked away from the window as he continued indoors.

She was nowhere to be seen and so he knelt before the TV in the lounge and began fiddling around with cables and plugs, eventually getting the VHS player setup. It sat far away from the main TV stand. He had dragged it out before everything else, the cables lying loose. He flipped on the TV and set it to the correct channel. He pressed in the button on the VHS player and heard a small whirr. He slid the tape into the player, watching as the words I BEG OF YOU TO HELP ME were dragged inside. He got up, stepped back, and perched himself on the edge of the sofa. Pressing PLAY on the remote and waiting.

At first nothing, some static. Then there appeared scenes from some old soap opera he didn't recognize. The audio was warped and the image faded and without tone. He thought maybe it was all a joke, and not just this, but everything, and so he slumped back into the sofa, internally giving up and externally huffing and throwing the remote to his side. The images on the screen flickered and the soap shopkeepers disappeared to reveal footage of an old man sat exactly where he now sat. The old man, who appeared to be at the limit of human age, sat as he had just done, perched on an old settee looking directly into the camera. The old man on the TV spoke calmly, without any affection or intonation or life, his eyes almost entirely sunken into his head. The longer the man watched, the easier he found it to outline the old man's skull. And so, the old man spoke.

*If you are watching this then I need your help. I need your help. I beg of you to help me. I have to begin from the beginning which I cannot truly remember, otherwise you won't know or understand any of it, and then I will be stuck here still longer. My name doesn't matter and after a time it fades anyway. But some time ago, a long time now, longer than anyone knows and longer than anyone will ever believe, I attempted suicide for the first time. I don't remember how old I was, but I was young, certainly, yes. I had had enough of living. I had always had enough of living. For as long as I can remember I have not wanted to remember or live or exist, and that hasn't changed. And so, it didn't take long for me to make the decision to not live and so I decided to hang myself. I went out to a tree some way away from anywhere and hung myself. I fell down, the rope cracked, and held me as a man hung. And yet I was alive. Gasping for air, in pain, but alive. I hanged there for roughly two weeks gasping for air until someone came across me. I guess they thought I had just done it and so ran over and propped me up and I got out of the noose, caught my breath, and then ran away. All the details of my life following this are hazy to me. But I estimate that I have attempted suicide well over 150 times via every means possible. Following my attempt at hanging, some months later, because I believed maybe this was a sign from God I went to church and all that and found nothing there, and so, I cut my wrists. I got in the bathtub with warm water just covering me and cut both wrists open. Over the course of hours, the bath eventually overflowed with my blood but I didn't even get the slightest bit dizzy. I remember standing up and draining the tub, and then, when the next day came my wrists held only a slight scar which quickly disappeared entirely.*

At this point in the video the old man went to scratch his leg. The old man moved slower than anyone he had seen, and for the first time the old man's clothes held to his body in a way that revealed his size. The old man was thin. Impossibly thin. Sitting up right under clothes that now seemed to hold him down. The old man returned to face the camera.

*After this I took up suicide attempts on a regular basis. Sometimes multiple times a week. It seems that I cannot break reality immensely, only enough to be considered a miracle time and time again. I remember jumping from a skyscraper and having both legs shattered upwards into my stomach only for the hospital to declare they somehow found me breathing and alive, and then fixed me some days later. The head doctor refused to come and see me leave. At most I felt a slight pain with those attempts. Mostly I feel chronic pain. I ache all over, everywhere. I am still rotting. I thought, after this, of so many attempts of rarer ways to end things, ways that maybe the universe could not reverse. This was how I discovered the place that's green, like a seafoam colour. I can't say much about it when I'm here. But it's between here and somewhere else and in the distance is a light not of yellow. A dark light that wants in. I can't say it's bad. The place is in-between here and elsewhere, yes. It isn't bad, but also isn't good. But there's comfort there and beings, but I can't speak of them. They know me now. I had tried to end it by way of a train. I stepped in front of it and it split me into pieces. That was when I first arrived there and found myself in a field of lilac grass looking up into an orange sky. I didn't even move because I felt more peace than I had ever felt before and didn't want it to end. Soon enough I awoke just beneath the bridge from under which I had run up to surprise the train. Years had passed and I had been declared missing. There were many times when things I did, attempts, got attention from papers or what not. I collected these clippings as evidence. I told many people about all this. But who would care? Who would believe? Soon enough I stopped trying to end it and got some jobs in some places that I can't remember now. But I still am a slave to time. I am a rotting man that can't die and I want to go to the other place for good. If you're watching this then, possibly, my idea worked. See, after I couldn't work due to being in so much pain I retired to where you now are. There I tried to figure a way to make it impossible for life to reinstate me, where any way I could gasp for anything was stopped, so then I could just stay in the other place, the place that's green, like seafoam. And this is where I am up to. I bought an old diving suit you see. What I will do is take the small boat out into the middle of the lake, the one a short walk from here that I hope you know of. And I plan to be wearing the bottom half of the suit already. I will row myself out into the middle of the lake and take with me masses of rope, blocks, cement, tape, and foam, like a spray foam that expands. I found some that works well, I can't remember what it's called. I tested a few things. I will tie all kinds of heavy blocks to me. I will then tape up the suit as well as I can, like you will have seen with the box this video will go in. I will be able to make up the cement on the boat and pour it into the bottom of the diving suit. From there I plan to fill my body via my throat with expanding foam. I will do this via the front of the diving suit and then, if I can, continue to fill the rest until life can no longer keep me and I float again into the other place. I will be all wrapped up, within a cocoon where life can't find me.*

The old man appeared sad now, as if he wanted to cry but his face would not let him. As he moved his head ever so slightly, his skin appeared paper thin.

*I am sorry but I beg of you. For if you have found this then yes, my plan has worked and I am still at the bottom of the lake in the suit. But if you are watching this and understand what I say then I ask something of you. To find me. If you believe all I have said, and if you come find me you truly will, then you may too understand that soon enough the lake will go dry, and there may then be no one around to help. I ask you to find me and release me fully. Take apart my suit and shred me. There is jewellery and many other things tucked away to pay for this. I pay my debts. The location of it is drawn on one of the papers in the box, it's not far and you can dig it up and buy what's needed. You have to shred me. Into pieces that are as small as possible. And then with those tiny pieces of me, throw me, handful by handful, into an oven or fire. And then, take that ash and try disintegrate it. This is my half-life wish. I ask that when you do this, you watch the whole process, try not to sleep. There is much money and jewellery to compensate you for this. Go there first and get that, and then come find me in the lake.*

With that the old man stood up and there seemed to be an almost indiscernible layer of dust that moved with him as he took his time stepping toward the camera. He swore he could hear the old man's aches. The video went back to the soap opera.

~

Well, what was on it then?

I didn't hear you come in.

I went for a walk. What was on it?

Some odd stuff, nothing to worry about though.

And what about the papers?

They're to do with it. I'll have to look at them again.

He stood up and knelt before the VHS player, feeling that he had no need to watch the video again, he understood the message and wanted nothing more than for it to not be true. And yet, as the old man had asked those who watched to come and find him, he knew also that his life was now haunted, that he now had an eternal itch, a debt, even. He took the tape out and stood up, turning to find his wife leant in the doorway. I hope you're going to tidy up that old player.

Not just now, I've got some stuff I have to do.

He walked back through to the kitchen and placed the tape back in the light green cloth. His wife followed him disapprovingly. I'm going for a walk, I'll be back in a while, he said, leaving the package on the table and swiftly exiting the kitchen. He knew the lake. He knew the lake exactly. Everyone knows if there's a lake nearby. And, soon enough, he was there, pushing his way through overgrown brambles as to stand before a decayed wooden jetty. He looked out over the lake, eyeing the bank all the way round for signs of a boat. There was nothing he could see. Then he eyed the centre and, holding his gaze onto a spot that held no meaning or worth for anyone at any time, knew it was all true, everything the old man said was true, and now it was only a matter of ignoring or paying a debt.

~

His wife merely stood by and made silent prayers during the days when he made trip after trip into the surrounding towns, bringing back various items and supplies. He comforted her by saying it was something he had to do. To which she would reply that they could just leave and not come back. But he would quickly be driving off again to buy something else. She stood in the kitchen mostly, and sometimes the garden, with her head lightly bowed muttering things to herself that only she felt the importance of. And, as it was always going to be, one day she awoke to find that he had left early to go someplace she didn't know specifically, but knew herself to be not good. She waited around in the house all day and knew this the day that could finally ruin it all, no prayer could hold against this, she thought and, as she thought this, dug her nails deep into her palm as to chastise herself. She went up to their bedroom and found the light green cloth package and brought it down. She found one paper that had a drawing on it of a map of their garden. She walked to a spot marked on it and found a deep hole. She walked back inside, sat at the kitchen table, and waited. She knew that no matter how much she understood of these papers and their details, she too would never understand, and she couldn't bear, not for a second, for her husband to enter into this, whatever it was.

Sometime after lunch she walked to the back door and looked out to find her husband stood in a wetsuit, drenched and tired. Holding some scuba gear with his hand he looked distraught. As he walked towards her, he said only that the body was sat upright and that the ropes snapped with ease. She only wanted not to know that which she now knew. Well, what are you going to do then?

I have to move the car as close as I can, I can't move him.

Do you need my help?

He's far too heavy, he said as he swiftly moved past her.

He reversed the car as close as he could and fastened a rope to the back. To her, he was out of sight, and so was what was to come. She saw only a rope get tenser and begin to move across the air, as if the rope itself was emanating from the direction of the lake. He got out and reattached the rope again, shortening the length as he ran out driving space. Again, she watched as it went from slack to tense and began to move. As she looked down the garden, just past a small fence, she saw the bracken and grass jolt and sway and bend. She heard a heavy rustling. A large object appeared and slowly cracked through the fence and into the garden. She watched as an old diving suit slid nearer to her. A hulking mass and tangle of canvas, copper, and trailing ropes. Looking upon this moving dead beast of weight she felt her lip quiver and stomach turn. Soon enough it was at the bottom of the garden some 20ft away, and then 10ft, and 5ft, and then, just over to her right was the fastened foot pressing against the house, causing the mechanical chimera arisen from the lake to jut and crack against itself, holding an artificial angle, the head was pushed as to look up at her. No eyes, no smile, no face, just a plain white bubbling of set foam. The suit fell back as the rope suddenly went slack, hitting the grass with a heavy thud. Just as she turned to go inside, she heard her husband cry out, Why didn't you tell me the old man had hit the house!

The diving suit laid next to the house. The wife was nowhere to be seen. The husband stood over it, looking down. The thick canvas jutted out at odd angles where the concrete had set. The ropes burrowed deep into the limbs. The helmet full with white. He sat for a while next to it. Holding his hand against the copper, and then brushing it down the canvas. He thought he heard a murmur, but he didn't know. He stood up and went into the lounge. He collapsed onto the sofa and fell asleep looking at the VHS player that his wife had place neatly onto the stand.

~

He awoke to yelling. Where'd you want this thing?

Around the back. He sat up and looked out of the front window, seeing that a bright red wood chipper had arrived. A man was leant against it talking to his wife. The man looked at him through the window and the wife followed suit. Late riser, eh!

He had a long day yesterday.

So, I just drive it down the side here? Looks like someone's been doing burnouts down there! he laughed and she didn't. The wood chipper man got in his van and drove around the side. The man, rushing through to the back, caught him as he pulled past the house. Anywhere here will be fine, he said, gesturing to the area just in front of the old man. Bit close to the house, 'nt it? the wood chipper man said leaning from his van window. Here will do nicely, the man reaffirmed.

Your money, the wood chipper man said as he leant back into his cab and positioned the wood chipper to where the man had pointed. The spout pointed down the garden. You'd best get everything organized, otherwise you're 'ole garden's gon be covered in chip! the wood chipper man said as he got out of his van. What in the hell you got there! Tha's 'n ol' diving suit, ent it?

Yeah, it's seen better days though.

What's that then, some kids fill the helmet with polystyrene or what?

Not sure, just something we found.

What you gon do with it?

Not sure yet.

I'd love me one of them, the wood chipper man said, walking closer to the suit. That really is a nice piece of gear, huh. Stood over it, admiring it, looking at each fold, the wood chipper man took a short step back and his eyes seemed to enter into a light trance, when one is looking dead ahead and knows it but can't seem to budge. The wood chipper man rubbed his stomach and looked sad. I really best be off and get out of your hair 'n all that. Hastily he walked over to the chipper and detached it.

So, how does it all work?

Ah, you'll figure it out, I'm sure. Just...just give the office a ring if there's any problems.

He stepped around and got into his van, winding up the window.

Thanks then.

But with that the wood chipper man was driving away.

~

From afar one would see, over the course of two-to-three hours, sparks flying from a tranquil garden, tugging and wrestling with old canvas, dust soaring high and disappearing into its own realm, and, if you were to keep your eyes on this scene with resolve and honesty, soon enough you would see a withered man-shaped spindle of skin be drawn from this mass of metal and weave, a misshapen globe of foam covering the place of the head. A being of a half-life appearing as some cosmic radiation victim caught in a chemical cloud, cursed to clutch to life to the last.

He kicked away all the debris from his grinding and cleared space for the old man. Grabbing a hammer and chisel he began to chip away at the foam, finding with surprise that after just a few knocks it cracked dead centre along its full length. He breathed in by mistake and tasted a forbidden vanilla in the back of his throat that made him wretch up acid. Before he could even think of his digestion, the foam cloud fell apart, revealing the face of the old man. The subtlest of grins with eyelids light, a contentment spoiled. For the grin turned to forced frown turned to grimace turned to the return of torture. Mouth opening of its own accord as a long streak of blackened foam arose from the old man's oesophagus and gently fell by his side, coated in a viscous browned jelly. The old man's mouth mushed shut, only for his lips to part to the size of a pea and, with a wheeze that wheezed itself, drew in anything it could find, as slow as a dying doe, as if his first breath now was his last again. The old man's eyelids quivered to slits, the eyeballs beneath rolling just. He's back, the man said to his wife. She had edged ever closer during the grinding procedure and now, unbeknownst to the man, stood at the old man's feet muttering meek prayers. We have to help him, she finally said aloud.

But I thought you-

By the mercy of the Lord I want him pulped!

Pulped?

I watched the tape. I know what he wants done to him and as I look at him now, it must be done, it must, it must!

Okay, well, let's take a break, rig up the chipper and go from there.

Okay. Would you like soup and a roll?

I think that would be nice right now.

~

The long-married couple sat at their kitchen table as such couple's do, without speaking any real words, only sporadically stating banal facts like We really must fix the vacuum cleaner, or The rolls are so much better when they're toasted, aren't they? And so, they sat in a silence filled with crap, which appears to be the only silence available since the fall. They finished their soups and rolls and teas and looked up at one another at what they must face. He looked to the right and she looked over her shoulder, out toward the back garden where, out of sight but never again out of mind, lay the cursed old man.

~

We'd best get this done, he said, as he pushed off from the kitchen table and strode quickly out the back. She followed with haste, not even clearing away the bowls. He told her, whilst looking down upon the old man, that he wanted this all done as quickly as possible. And so, after giving the chipper a once-over, checking the bag was securely fastened, and checking once that it ran smoothly, he thought of the logistics. Standing over an abomination of the cosmos, figuring out how best to pulp it. That new soup is quite good, she said.

Head first, he said.

He once again started the chipper and allowed it to run for a minute or so, thinking this would allow it to breathe or some such. The deep mechanical roar seeming to vibrate the leaves of the surrounding trees. All the while he didn't take his eyes off the old man, managing once or twice to witness a flicker of muscle. Eventually he took a deep breath and squatted, preparing himself to pick up the weight of a human being. He grasped the arms of the old man on either side, pushing them into his emaciated torso as one would bundle up a bunch of large sticks. And, pressing off hard with his legs, shot up far faster than he thought. As if one prepared to grab a mug full of coffee that they forgot was empty, the vessel shooting upward quick and one is surprised at just how much force they use throughout the day. The same here too, for he shot up and spontaneously used the opportunity to boost the old man onto his left shoulder. The old man held parallel to the floor like some old worn plank. He then proceeded to press the old man upward with both his arms, above his head, appearing to offer him back to the great chasm itself. Holding this abortion of mortality aloft, he took the few steps over to the chipper and prepared to tilt the old man into the opening. Once again taking a deep breath, which caused him to taste the admittedly good tomato soup he'd just eaten, he went to tip the old man head first into the chipper. He noticed his wife in the corner of his vision, smiling, happy with an honest beaming smile. He looked upward at the face of the old man as he tilted him into the chipper. He expected, despite all he knew, for this life to scream back at him for giving it an end, but all he saw was all the old man's skin droop down his body, covering his entire face like a waterfall of plastic rot. With that he dropped him, quickly stepped back, and watched as that universally incorrect plank of blackened flesh was drawn into the shredder and mulched to pieces. The chipper bag quickly getting heavier and heavier. Soon enough the last inch of the old man from the video tape had disappeared into the chipper and been transmuted into fine pieces of threshed flesh. He pushed a few stray bits of wood through the chipper to be sure that all the man was gone. A smell of dank wood and mothballs hung in the air.

Smells like my grandma's old bedroom, she said.

And mine, he said. Anyway, quickly open that bag and keep your eyes on it.

Okay, she said.

He quickly ran and grabbed a large tarp and placed in on the lawn. It held perfectly still, and for the first time, he noticed that there wasn't even a hint of wind. Okay, you grab that end and I'll take this one. The two of them moved the bag onto the tarp. He opened it and quickly tipped the contents out, hastily spreading it around with his feet. Okay, he said to his wife, what I need you to do is to spread this out as thin as possible so it at least has some chance of being dry. I'm going to build a fire. And so, he built a fire, and she spread the pulp over the tarp with her feet. As she did so she couldn't help thinking about butter on scones. Soon enough the fire was burning, helping the light of the sun dry the remains of the old man.

Okay, we'll sit here tonight and keep an eye on it all, and then in the morning we'll brush it into a pile into the centre and throw the entire tarp into the fire, okay?

Sounds great, she said, as she sat cross-legged on one side of the tarp.

Are you going to need to sleep?

I don't think so, she said, that soup will keep me going.

Okay, well I'm going to go make a flask of coffee to keep us sharp.

That sounds lovely, dear.

~

They sat, this long-married couple, either side of the tarp, each now with their respective cups of coffee in hand, the flask leaning against his knee. The sun had long since set, the darkness never truly arrived, and they had been left within the twilight. She would occasionally look up at him and smirk, bowing her head back down before he had time to catch her. He would do much the same, and so neither ever noticed how much the other loved them. He finished up his last cup of coffee, patted his belly, and leant on his side, with his head on his hand, admiring his wife. She politely sipped her final cup, looking back at the house and thinking it might be time to re-do the kitchen. The sun finally awoke from atop the trees and cast small shadows off the old man spread thin.

~

Okay, he said, if you go grab the cans of petrol from over there, I'll get some more logs on the fire and get it ripping. Also, once you get the cans, go grab the tape and the papers and lob them onto the tarp! So, she rushed off to grab the cans and the tape and the papers whilst he piled logs onto the fire. Making sure that after each log he looked back upon the tarp. She returned with the cans and automatically sat back down where she had been, gazing into and over the tarp. He decanted the petrol into some buckets that lay nearby and placed them a few steps away. She pushed herself back a little, noticing that he was ready to sort out the tarp. I think I'll be okay to do this myself, he said, I think it will be quicker.

I think so too, she said.

And so, he roughly brushed the dried pulp that lay near the outside into the centre with his foot. Then, he quickly gathered up all four corners of the tarp and slung it over his shoulder like some travelling cannibal gourmand. With a single, tranquil heave he swung the cursed knapsack into the fire and jogged to the buckets of petrol. One by one he lobbed each bucket quite literally into the fire, caring not for the buckets themselves. The fire soared and burned the branches that hung over it some way up. The tarp had quickly melted. The man peered deep into the fire, his face growing hot and red, witnessing as each piece of pulp disintegrated and was carried high into the air as a quickly forgotten ash. He stood like this for some time, his eyebrows singed and eyes profusely watering. And he stood until the end, as was his debt. Until the fire was but embers and, as far as his gut and heart could tell him, not a speck of the wrong remained.

~

Some weeks passed by and the only reminders left were the chipper, which the wood chipper man had never come to pick up, the grassless circle where the fire had been, which in time would be once again green, and their memories, which would never again be right. In the evenings they would sit in the garden, each with their own camping chair. They would sit just outside the back door and look out toward the lake. A bottle of wine, maybe, or even a late flask of tea. They would speak of deeper things and found a lot of peace just being together. He knew she had been checking. She knew he had been checking too. And, amidst their peace, both would look at one another and know the other knew. One night she turned and said, The leaves, they're mottled black.

Yes, I know. But what can one do?

# Yeah, it's okay, I'll wait in the car

I'm just going to pop in the shop, do you want to come with me or do you want to wait here?

I'll wait here.

Are you sure?

Yeah, it's okay, I'll wait in the car.

But have you ever waited in the back of a car, no philosopher could touch that time, touch that space. There is nothing there for anyone and for a child it is their first glimpse toward all the things that are anathema to childhood and life itself. Silence, patience, nothing. But even then, the patience fades away, not into an impatience, not even into a submission; one becomes as apathetic as the tarmac, an apathy void of passivity.

First you check the large pockets on the back of the front seats for any magazines or leaflets or maps, even, but when you pull out the inevitable repetitions you have handled many times before you are handed over to the fact of this repetition and just sigh and put them back. Yet even so, once they are back in, they are out again, not for reading or studying, just for looking at, flicking through, going over, an object to hold your attention, to stop your mind from drifting away. But time doesn't work that way here and she or he will be gone maybe 15 maybe 40 and yet it will be longer, it's always longer, but you won't accept it, not now, not ever.

You could stare at the people and cars and animals outside the windows, even the sway of the trees, but you can't, because the smears and grease and smudges and dirt of the windows is extant enough to close you in. And so now all those things are out there and you are in here and that's how it is. Sure, it's static, and the air is recycled and it gets stuffy. But it isn't that. This is the truth of existence allowed those hardly born. You sit and wait and nothing shall come of it and your experience of it is not acknowledged and you drive away, sliding back into the slow hue.

Sometimes you sit there and everything is far away even if close, and a friend might walk by, a friend from school. But no one ever sees anyone waiting in a car, especially in the back seat. There are people out there having conversations and you hear the words but can't make out the discussion, it's all lost so quickly. No one wants to admit that though, how quickly it all goes. And then you push your head back into the headrest, or even lean right over and lay down on the seat, and you feel it's kind of grubby and bring yourself back up and understand you have to be upright to wait, there isn't a way out of this. And that's it, that's why it actually hurts, all of this, not only is there no way out, but you're made to sit upright the entire time.

And now there is nowhere to go and nothing to do; time itself is a waste of time. And now your friends who pass by are getting older and you wonder if a couple of the far away people are your parents. And your neighbour stands in front of the car and looks confused and older than you remember. You pull out the magazine and map again, they might as well not exist, but you hold onto them and flick through as you look elsewhere. And it's getting dark now. Not pitch black, that would mean something else. But the twilight is here and belated workers arrive to pick up a quick dinner. They are quiet. Some of them sit in their cars for a bit before going into the store. Not in the same way I sit here though, they are taking a break and I am here in the first of all breaks, the one that will come to haunt me, but I don't know that now.

Sorry I was gone so long, everything okay?

Yeah.

But it isn't, and it never will be again. As we pull away the weight of nothingness comes with me and I'm still there, held there. I miss the people who walked by, who I saw. I miss the peace of that place, maybe there's peace enough in purgatory alone? Anything that is different to this existence must be peace of a sort. As if one had stood for days, even weeks, and then finally been given a seat. You never think you'll get up again. Like having a deep flu that leaves you at some mercy you didn't know, the acceptance found there, maybe.

Later in school, days maybe, weeks? I'm still there really, and everything's getting done but, I'm still there. And I know I can't return on a whim, that place couldn't be made. It's more than a zone or a phase. You can't make the in-between. I'll be there again, I know it, forgotten once again, some place, somewhere. People are chatting around me now and all I can think of is that place. There was a bliss. A bliss of neutrality. No act there had potency. There was no act, even. Just, nothing. And I miss it. What it is to be completely forgotten, even if for a moment.

I wouldn't like a gravestone, nothing that lasts. At most I want a piece of wood with a name lazily carved. Then I can die with the knowledge that all traces of me will cease to exist, and maybe when it all comes to pass, time itself will forget me. One can only hope.

# Some People Livin Just Ain't Made For Life

Old Billy wasn't even old when I spoke to him, 45 he was, and he, as they say, had received the worst of it from this here world. See now, Billy, often pronounced Bill-eh, had been one of those thin half-emaciated kids that smelt faintly or urine or bleach or both. The kind of kid that even those with warm hearts couldn't bring themselves to talk to or humour. Hell, there wasn't anything wrong with him back then, he wasn't necessarily weird, though certainly became so in time, maybe, but he didn't have many friends, he ate a weird lunch, and played weird games, but there wasn't anything truly off-putting about him. But either way, any way you shook it, in fact, Billy was an odd one and I can't imagine anything he could have done would have warmed anyone or anything to him. An unexciting curse sent down from the cosmos, not streaked with black or sulphur, nor even what one might call an exciting psychopath, no, nah, young Billy (who become Old Billeh) was just that kid, and that kid will always be that kid, and there's places in all playgrounds and all workplaces and even in the smallest of bus stops for such kids to sit or stand. He didn't feel sorry for himself and no one felt any pity for him, hell, most of the time you wouldn't even know young Billy (and in turn Old Billeh) even existed. He didn't seem to mind, hell, I'm not sure he even knew he existed back then or even now. And the time passed like it does, and it did for Billy too, perhaps slower for him, though I can't be sure. Some of us remember him out of the corner of our eyes, slumped somewhere, sat or stood he was slumped, weighing thin and heavy and insignificant under his hand me down clothes that, even if the most prestigious tailor took the time to fit them would refuse to fit such a body. It can't be helped, such a curse, some people living just ain't made for life. I wish it were, you know? I wish it was that everyone fit in, that everyone found some group they truly fit in to, that it was made mandatory that every person made to live was equally made to find their soulmate, but that just ain't so, far from it. Most people live as if in a known half-life, they know it to be true that they were born with a gape and will never be full, but they accept it and move on as it's best to do. Anyway, back to Billy. You know, he never did get rid of that grease in his hair, or the pointy boney structure of his body, or the fact he somehow always bought really thick-soled shoes that looked like something a pilgrim had sent him from the past. Truly, a urine-tainted, weedy, weepy, perpetually coughing, trembler if there ever was one. But hell, unlike many others, you had to give it to young and old Billy because he did keep going. He made it out of school alive. In fact, I believe he made it out with little to no bullying, maybe because he really was just nothing at all, I don't know. But he got out all the same and, if I remember right, he didn't fancy college or any more education, not because he disliked school, for he couldn't really remember it, even immediately after the fact, but because he had no clue what to do with himself because he never felt himself to be anyone at all. And, as such people who can't believe they're really people are wont to do, he accepted the first job given to him. Hell, it wasn't even given to him, he just happened to be forced into conversation with some loud-mouthed family friend whilst walking in town and they told him about the job and then said he should apply and then said they were in charge and then said his Dad had asked them about the job *for* him and then told him that if he got to the job site at 8am on the Monday it was his and then took a twenty from their pocket and gave it to him, Billy, for boots and then, walking away, said that they would see him Monday bright and early. Billy, as he was, that kid, that kind of person who life takes for a ride like some kind of test subject, just said yes. Hell, not even a real affirmative yes, not a yes that meant yes at all, maybe an acknowledgement, maybe, but he said yes like a little baby boy and felt he might be that kid forever, and, even so, any choice and all decision aside, knew he'd be there at 8am on Monday, and of course, he was. The job was groundskeeping, nothing, really. Some government funded park where certain kids of Billy's kind ended up and pushed around various wheelbarrows of cut branches and mud all day and seemed to do a lot and nothing at all at once. Sure, one could say that the parks were tidy and clean and well-kept and friendly and pleasant and all of that stuff. But when you met the people in charge of such acts, well, those supposedly in charge of such acts, you could only conclude that such virtues had little, if nothing, to do with them, and that, in truth, they were employed only to stop people realizing that the purest and best things in all existence were those that no human being had ever laid a finger upon. And so, Billy walked around the park doing this or that, trimming that which would grow back, scraping scum from where it would reappear, raking away the dead foliage of a season yet to come, a job of decay by a soul forgotten already. He did that for some years and at some point in there he met a girl. Well, he didn't exactly meet a girl, see when he was working, she just happened to be put on my team and he didn't think much of it, Dorine her name was. He told me that even then he remembered thinking that Dorine was an old-fashioned name and that he got the sense that when one is cursed with a truly old name it sinks into their being and they never really feel young, as if they're waiting around for an age when it will make sense why they were ever named such. Of course, the time comes and one is none the wiser and then one dies anyway. Even he noticed that she walked almost with a forward lean as if something was aching or at least ready to ache within her. It was some six months to a year before they spoke properly. Before then he had just occasionally told her it was lunchtime or where she should be cutting or where the tool she needed was. But as it was, and as it happens, and as it happened for young adult Billy, she one day asked him what he liked to do after work. Billy had never been asked such a thing and so he said they really should get on and walked away. But, as it also happens, such kids like Billy get these weird little spurts of confidence like apologies from God and the very next day he went up to her and said that he Didn't do much of anything after work, why? To which she replied that Well, she was just wondering. Oh, he said, how long have you worked here? to which she replied, Well I've only been on your team since I started, but I guess that's what? Like a year or so now? And here's the thing, and he told me this, and it might be the one thing that could ever make me smile, from nowhere, like some voice that he always wished he'd had, a self that could wash away that faint urine smell and weakness and loathsome meekness, out of the strangest blue he said to Dorine You know, I quite like having you on my team, would ever like to maybe come with me after to work for a drink or something like that possibly? And he told me that all came out in one blurt and she had this odd cute smile like she'd been waiting for him to say *anything* like that for years, even though she'd only known him for one, but either way, her old heart leapt high because she knew she always wanted to hear that, and had always wanted to hear just that from just him. A moment that, for her, simply *was.* And if it hadn't been, well, surely that'd have meant a complete submission to the name of Dorine and a long agonizing and loveless life of the coldest asceticism. And so it was, as you can imagine and I full well know, they dated and shared rides and shared lunches and had much youthful sex and moved in together and got a cat and he proposed (on one knee) and she accepted (crying) and the wedding was cheap and unspokenly bleak and dull and they were together for a year or two and they got a mortgage and she got pregnant and had twins (a boy and girl) and they were happy for a couple of years or so, but then, before long, something better from the great nothingness of the bitter better comes in and shits across the sky, those were his thoughts when just after the kid's (who were not weird at all) second birthdays she said she wanted a divorce. He didn't make her happy, it wasn't him it was her, we want different things, things have changed, it's best for the kids; it didn't matter he thought and she thought, it was coming and they both knew it, baked into his childhood and her name were misery. And so, they got divorced and she became truly happy, hell, even a bottle of cheap wine seemed thereafter to make her genuinely happy. And he retreated into himself, to the self that he couldn't avoid. And, as they'd both remained as groundskeepers, he felt shunned and slowly retreated, eventually leaving and taking up a job on a construction site. Some years down the line and I heard that she's now met some other guy from the groundskeeping place, some guy that had been working there ages and who she occasionally used to take her lunch with. I left her to it. I see the kids now again, once a month or so. I don't think it's that they don't want to see me, but that really, I have nothing to offer them. I could give them all the gadgets and whatever they want, hell, I don't do anything with my money, but that isn't what they want, I can sense that at least, but that doesn't mean I can figure out what it is they want. So, we see each other and we don't really talk but I like to see them all the same, but I can't help feeling they're bored. Anyway, the reason I'm here is, the other day, Tuesday just after lunch, which is my least favourite time of all, I was on the construction site and two guys were off ill so I was working my ass off carrying bricks and doing the most repetitive work you can imagine. Anyway, the reason I'm here is, see, it started to rain, like in those old movies where they haven't got it quite right yet and it's absolutely pouring, you get soaked in seconds and are truly wet through, your bones are cold through and you know it'll be two or three days until you are really warm again. Anyway, the reason, the reason I'm here is, I'm stood there in that rain, utterly miserable, despair beyond any weight imaginable, the cosmos of death and all depression pouring down in each drop, and with each of those drops I am vividly reminded of my position in all this, and I reminded of everything I told you of just now, how I am Billy and Billeh, how I am *that* kid, and how I stank of urine and still stink of urine and Dorine and the kids and everything you know, everything you know and can surmise from this about me, from this and all our other past sessions, and the reason I'm here is, the reason I had to tell you all this is, I'm stood there in that stupid ridiculous rain on that Tuesday afternoon, and it's pouring down, soaking me, and all of this comes back to me over and over and over and over and over and over again with each drop vivid as if it were all happening all at once right now, and I'm stood there and the reason I'm here is, I'm stood there, in all *that,* and, and...I get the hardest fucking erection of my life? What's that about?

# The Townplace

And they were then going to go on a holiday, on a break, on a well-deserved vacation as people then were wont to do. To *get away* they said to themselves, drawing it into a prophecy, a revelation almost. Every once in a while, we all go away for a bit and then come back and most often nothing changes in itself at all, but if it were to change, and sometimes it apparently does...can you blame them? Can you blame anyone?

They'd been saving up all their coppers and coins and so each paycheque took a little hit that stung with a sweetness, but they thought of their children and went to bed without even a memory of indigestion. Two they'd had, jolly kids, well-behaved by all accounts, not an ounce of sadness, not in this world, I beg it, and it became true.

He'd been there when he too was a child, where they are going that is, and as it was that they had found each other, she had since heard him speak of it so, a lift of the eyes into the past as if it could erase the days that had hurt since. A little place way out there, beyond the tumult and tumble, a place where even weeds ached nicely and skies were forever forgiving, maybe, but then there can't be hesitation.

And the day would come when they'd pack up their things into rarely used bags and rucksacks that held crisp crinkles and faded folds. The little one took her teddy called Ted who had seen better days. They clipped him into the middle seat and she giggled and grinned with an actual joy, her brother too was happy that she was happy, patting little Ted on his worn and scraggy head. The car pulling away with the warmth of a new beginning that offered the good alone, and we all hope it will be right for them, but can anything hold together for people of such grace.

The car trundled outward from their hamlet. Past the forgettable towns where textures repeated and conversation followed suit. Past the piece of woodland that was year-round allergic to green. Onto a motorway that was only an extension, becoming as it soared. And they soared too, one with the road for a while as those in the front were as young as those in the back and you couldn't say if a thing at all mattered, but there was a beauty there, not hidden away, but out in front for those who wished to look and see.

Into the little getaway that had already carved out a space for it to be remembered, with an attention like none other, as if each passing blur held weight against the expanse they'd left behind. And tiny Ted with the scraggy head sat still the whole journey, with the other little one checking in on him every once in a while, and the brother checking on her, and the mother on him, and the father on her, and then a chasm admitted to by the last in line, if he so wished, but then it could all fall down, so he turned back only to the road, his eyes half bleary from sleep.

And the road did carry them with that old car trundling along as a fellow member of the crew. Even the sun flickering between the branches could not annoy the delicate transience owed. Soon enough the little one fell asleep, the brother followed her into the dream, and the mother too after checking in on them, casting a glance to wide-eyed Ted who himself appeared happy to keep watch. The father awake and at the wheel thought solely of the destination, the journey was for them and could be left with a heavy sigh for their dreams alone. He couldn't help but feel the only thing he didn't want to feel, meaning the day had become spoiled in an instant. Like a little baby bird screeching for its mother whilst one says their vows, but what one can do, and so he held to the wheel and thought on it and thought back.

There was a time when things were right, and that time had a place, and what a risk it is to take oneself back there after some duration. He had broached other sights and other spaces to find often they were less vibrant and usually far smaller, not one had lived up to the standard of his memory, let alone heart. But this is one he had to share, just a town, no place truly special, and yet a place, for him, held together by threads of quick smiles and innocent friendships, each road holding only joy, whimsy, even. What a risk, but then, what a tyranny to not take those he loved the most to the place that had loved him the most. They'd arrive soon enough however, and so as is the case with these things, he was left alone with nothing to do but be alone at the only time he wanted otherwise. But what can one do? Life never promised a thing, and all yearning, all hope, all love, all joy, and even all of that happiness is resting upon the notion of a promise never made.

And the time comes when the repetitive gives way to the familiar and one finds themselves folded into another atmosphere, invited or not. He knew the roads now and with that knowledge came all other attachments. That is where Peter fell in the mud. That is where Phil lost his shoe. That is where they chased the squirrel. That is where they came up with the name of their group. That is where he realized he had a crush. And that is where before you know it you have arrived. No one has ever been arrival ready. To separate wheat and chaff is to separate those who can comport themselves quickly after arrival, but he stayed half vacant and listened for any signs of stirring in the back to allow himself avoidance, because maybe it will not be alive anymore.

And soon enough they did stir. First the mother, who stirred them both, and the little one's tired arm bumped Ted on his scraggy head. The yawns all settled and they found themselves bumping up a long drive and then parked up outside a hotel with all white walls. They used to be wooden doors and windows, but not so much has changed. He stepped out into the gravel and stretched deep, with a release that left him unnervingly in need of his wife's voice. I'm right here. He looked up at the hotel as he heard sister and brother scuttle in the gravel. Soon enough the little one was next to him holding Ted, turning his scraggy head to look up at the hotel. That's where we'll be staying! Oh wow! It's really nice. It's been a while.

But he, the father, the father of it all, had to admit, it had been too much of a while and that perhaps it would all come back and it all would turn out to be nothing after all, and what could he really do to protect them? Not from violence, not from hostility, not even from aggression, but from the sole fact that so many things and people and friendships turn into that which one calls banal and nothing and that, in the end, there is little more depressing that witnessing a friend who was really and totally true transform before one's eyes into just another of them all, one of the mass to be forgotten.

And as he stood by the car, the night arriving in an hour or so, he turned to his wife and, looking over the car into her eyes and into a past she knew of yet had not experienced, told her that he would be back later. He stepped away from the car and the young daughter all happy and young looked back at him, he stood hesitant, ready to turn away. Oh, I'm okay! he said to the little ones, it's just been a while since I've been here, this is where Daddy grew up! They looked up at him excited and he looked down at them with a fear they couldn't recognize. He looked up once more at his wife, and how much he loved her was recognized in a single look, but then memories of childhood and teenage youth might usurp all given a chance, and so without a kiss or hug he turned and went to walk into town.

And as he walked down the driveway, he felt everything fade away as before him he noticed that even how the trees bowed had memory. Onto the path and to the right again the road soared onward and seemingly upward into his old town, with a little look to the right he saw that the walls all cobbled and concrete with ivy and dark mud stayed true to his memory, at least something held, he thought. And atop them were bushes and short trees and well-kept fences. And across the road was well kept grass and edged-paths and post boxes painted fresh red, lampposts freshly changed with light from right outside the case. Everything seemed right as he walked toward memory. But memory is only ever memory of memory, and to carry that on ad infinitum, well, what can memory be at all after a year or two, a wish, a memory desired? Nothing at all?

In time, a short time, too short, really, he was there, the space his desire had guarded for so long. Not an inch was incorrect. He looked upon the town square and, empirically, not a jot had changed. The signs and lettering and gutters and ambience and noise and litter, all the same, not a morsel of the life that was before was different, but he felt and knew that he didn't belong. He'd been here and he'd been there and everywhere he looked he had an exact recollection. This place could be recreated from his memory, but from that creation would only be a half-life, nothing of now would exist, as it had long lived without him and he knew it. Sure, he'd stood in that phone box and sat on that bench and been in that shop and drunk at that pub and been a regular at that bar, years he could see, running before him, but they were gone. Jimmy! Damn! I thought that was you! How you been?

~

Dean?

Jimmy!

Dean.

Jimmy!

Dean. Yeah, how you been? What you been up to?

You know, this n that, you know how it is. You?

Well, wife and kids, just down here for the weekend really.

You got a wife? I bet she's a catch. And kids two, what's that like girl n boy or...?

Oh, a boy and a girl-

I bet your wife's a catch...she a fitty, hotty...knowing you she is, you remember that time it was me, you, Caz, and Phil under the bridge?

Yeah, she's...she's my wife. Yeah, I remember that night, what were we, 19? What'd that be now, say 20 years ago?

I dunno man, maybe, what a fuckin night though, Phil and his shoe. Say! I'm off down the *G 'nd G* tonight and I guess a few of em will be up there...come with me!

Well, I was just walking really-

Nah, man, Jimmy, you've *got to*, come on, just for one, come on, it's the *G*, just for one, Jimmy, come on!

Alright, alright Dean, sure sure, I'll come down there. Man...it's been a while though. How've you been?

I knew you would. I knew *you* would, you're an old buh ain't ya! Aye aye come on then!

Sure, wait up. But Dean was rushing off with a stride that had haste but appeared entirely normal for his legs. Dean strode and strode as the plain Jimmy and pleasant family of Jimmy and the memory of the family vacation faded and faded. Dean! he half launched his voice a bit ahead to try slow Dean down. Dean looked back. Jimmy, fuckin' come on, let's have a few, like old times, like old times, me and you Jimmy, like me and you James, like me and you Jim, like me and you Tim, lime me and you Jimmy! he said, everywhere and all at once and drifting away. Alright alright I'm coming.

Aye, yeah, that's the empty sentence, alright alright, I'm coming I'm coming, the after thought, I'll see you there, I'll see you there!

Dean! Dean! It's 7pm! Dean...Dean it ain't even 8! But then, he was already far ahead and wasn't with our family man. He tried to muster the strength, the motivation, to pick up the pace and catch up to his old friend who was fast disappearing into the half-light. Soon enough he found himself fully immersed and fully alone in a place he thought would have died by now. His old friend was gone.

He knew where he was. But everything was gone. He knew where he was and, he said to himself, that he'd always know where he is here. There's not a foot of land he doesn't have a clumsy nostalgic claim to, not a bench he hadn't squandered hours upon. He knew it was a few more steps, then a left through a rarely used carpark, then across a small patch of grass, and then, finally, to the right would be an alleyway looking down to a kebab or chip or pizza shop, he knew it would be one of those. His legs took him there as his mind struggled in its own grey quagmire.

And, soon enough, as it is with such places and such habits, he found himself there. He had found himself, there, once more. He looked it over, the old bar. It hadn't changed. A new coat of paint, the same colour as before. New benches, same as the last. Old patrons. He knew a few of those standing outside before he could even make them out, their presence was enough for him to know who they were. Jimmy! There he is boys! He walked over not of his own accord.

He stood and made all the expressions he needed to. He heard the stories he'd always heard. They were as excited and angry and frustrated and lecherous and drunk as they had been before. It had been years. He looked at them one by one and they were gone. Nothing behind them. Laughter all automatic. Hand movements all rehearsed. Jimmy was all looking about with a sincerity not meant for there and Dean, in the middle of a story concerning a lost shoe, turned swift to Jimmy, his great donkey grin plummeting and glared at the bridge of his nose deep. Don't do that Jim, he said with force and the apparent agreement of the atmosphere. The noise rose back up and the smog returned and he was left to fend for himself. He decided to walk home.

He left the front of the pub and made the decision to go back through town on his way back to his family. He would go past all the old shops and the barbers and the bakers and even catch a glimpse of the old school. However, he found himself sat on a bench in the middle of the town looking out upon all the cardboard buildings. The music from the pub seemed to rush and die, rush and die, rush and die, until finally it ebbed out. This happened in a trance for him, and all that passed him by was two people and an old cat. As the noise fell away the voices loomed from where he had been. It was his old friends, still there, just stood, like they had been an unknown amount of time ago.

He looked down at his feet and pushed himself off the bench. Arching up he found passing him by and coming back and closer were his old friends, but their faces didn't make sense to him. As if someone had nudged them back a bit or knocked them off centre, their faces just didn't sit right and none of the muscles seemed to pull. Oh, where'd you bloody well go then Jimmo? one of them said in a single monotonous sentence. Yeah Jimm-o, where did you go? said another whose voice seemed to come from far behind him. And I did tell you not to do it didn't I Jimmy, I did say, said Dean, as he lifted his chin a little to look up past him, as if to see through him into his future. The others held places around him both too close and too far away, five there were now. He recognized them all but they didn't hold their true names. They all held him in their sights and had not a clue what to do with him. Jimmy felt put out. One of them wiped their runny nose and one let out a single shrill cough like a backfiring engine. Say Jimmy, do you happen to remember the time with the lost shoe? said Dean, spoken from the depths of his gut with his great grin from hell reaching in every direction. Just tell me that, Dean said, just tell us all that you remember that and it's there with you, up there, Dean said, lightly pushing his finger into Jimmy's forehead a little dribble of thin spit fell from his mouth.

Sure Dean, I remember.

And you will always remember?

Sure, Dean.

It was funny, wasn't it, when he lost the shoe?

Yeah Dean, sure was.

It's been good to have you back here Jimmy, and we're all glad you remember. We have to get back to it now, you know. But we all wonder what you're going to do now?

I'm going to home tonight, Dean, though I may be around town in the day.

Oh, okay Jimmy.

Dean stepped back, keeping his eyes on the spot just behind Jimmy. Dean's eyes were sullen and drooped with sadness. Dean turned and walked off, appearing to dissipate into an alleyway, the others leaving only as already forgotten footsteps. Jimmy looked around into the flat nothingness and found little held his attention. He began walking back. Looking into shop windows and lounge windows, over hedgerows and into cars. One street before home he turned to look behind him and saw the faint resemblance of a figure, held all fuzzy in the middle of the street some way away. It looked up at him and half-bowed its head, walking away into the night. He arrived home where it was all quiet, he felt there was a peace upstairs that he shouldn't disturb, and so he sat and fell asleep on the sofa.

~

He awoke before them, early. He left a note that said he had gone into town and would be back soon. He didn't feel groggy or bleary or tired, he felt plain, like everything had been done. He walked directly to town, noticing as he walked some other old memories that now appeared as they hadn't before. He got to the town and saw that it was busy. A market day. Little stalls and small talk and short steps, everyone bumbling about, no one really there. He looked at the bench from last night and then looked over to the alleyway where Dean had exited into. He took nothing from this. He looked around the market place and caught a woman on the other side of the square looking directly at him but he couldn't make out her face. He went to step toward her but something stopped him. He tried again and she walked away. The woman in the bakery and the customers she was serving all seemed to look out at him. He looked back and they all stared at each other for a while. He walked over and into the store. Could I get these please he said, handing the woman a pack of four bread rolls.

Okay, she said.

Before he or they knew it, the transaction was done, and he was outside the store again looking in, and then back where he was, bread rolls in hand. The old cat passed by his feet, heading in the opposite direction from last night, he watched as it left his sight. He looked around one final time and accepted that he couldn't really see anything, and perhaps they saw that he couldn't see, and so he headed home.

~

I just saw your note love! How was town?

Yeah, it was okay, just got us some rolls for breakfast.

Oh, that's lovely, his wife said, giving him a little lovely loving peck on the cheek.

Are the kids up?

Oh, likely not! I let them stay up and watch a scary movie.

Sounds like a fun night.

It was spoooookkkyyy! she said, waggling her fingers and raising her eyebrows at him as if to mimic a silly ghost. What about you, how was your night? Didn't get in too much trouble, I hope?

No, nothing like that. Did end up down the *G 'nd G* for a bit, but didn't drink any.

The *G 'nd G*, now there's a name I haven't heard in years! How was it? Any of the *old crew* down there? she said sarcastically.

Yeah, a couple...a few.

Let me guess, Dean was about?

Yeah. Dean was there.

And...how is old Dean?

He's fine, hasn't changed really.

That doesn't surprise me. Let me guess, he kept trying to tell that story about the time Phil lost his shoe! she said, walking away into the kitchen with the bread rolls.

He did, he said.

# After All Things, Maybe.

and like everyone, at least, I imagine everyone else does this, I fantasize about my funeral. Not in any specific sense, there aren't any specifics to this fantasy, I don't want to know if certain people will come or how many people attend or what will be said of me, at least I think I don't, but really, I just want to know what it's going to be like. Even if only a few people, even just a handful, turn up, then I still just want to know what it will be like, and I imagine what it, that is, my funeral, will be like *all the time*. I sit in the same chair that I always sit in at nighttime, night after night, a rugged computer chair that swivels, and I fantasize about my funeral. The event we all wish we could attend, at least, I imagine everyone wishes they could attend, and the one event we evidently cannot. And I imagine that as the funeral crowd, perhaps just a handful, maybe even less, get up to leave that the priest beckons them down, beckons them back to their seats, which in my imagination are hard, old pews, and the crowd are sort of disgruntled at the fact they have to come back and sit down again, acknowledging how numb all their asses are. My dear friends, he says, in my imagination, one more thing! I know this is not the norm, but he, this is the priest speaking of myself from my imagination, asked me explicitly to read this to you all *after all things*, that is, at the true end of the funeral. These terms, *after all things* and *the true end of the funeral* have a great ring for me, and in my imagination, I imagine that the priest, who speaks to the crowd very solemnly and sincerely, really manages to convey the weight of these terms, especially *after all things*. In my imagination, I feel that if the priest doesn't manage to capture the heavy rhythm of *after all things*, then the funeral shall be a failure. He, this is the imagined priest once more talking about myself, said to me, explicitly, that the time to read this, to announce this, will be when they are all just about to rise. And so, I ask you all, now, to once again take your seats for *the final thing he wanted you to hear*, this is what he said to me, and—producing some sheets of paper from his inside pocket—this is the last thing he, once again the priest, imagined, talking about me, wanted you to hear. The priest will be very solemn and sincere here, if he doesn't unfold the paper correctly or ruffles it or it catches on his clothes or he doubles-up a word or some such other piece of unseriousness, well, then, the whole thing is a sham and a failure and should really just be forgotten. And, before we get to what is written by myself and read out by the priest at my imagined funeral, I have to add that, during many of my recent imaginings of the said funeral, sometimes I happen to imagine that the priest does mess up, or someone in the crowd coughs at the wrong time, or a truck blares past, or even sometimes that the priest forgets to read it or gets the timings wrong or reads it all out in some horrid monotone voice that just takes the weight away, and so it's here, right now, that I have to get my imagined funeral and its proceedings out in the fresh air, because otherwise I am left only with this half-failed, half-successful funeral in my mind. And so, when we look back at the funeral, we remember that the priest, all solemn and sincere, had just removed the paper from his pocket, with a precise movement, very focused in his actions, and he clears his throat, but not too much, it's not ridiculous and certainly doesn't go in for a second clearance of his throat lest he ends up sounding like some spluttering old fool, it's a quick clearance because he's assured in himself of how important it was for me for this to be read, and, I made sure to tell him so before I died just how importance it was. And so, he begins his reading, clear precise words with the right inflections and intonations and tone...

*I wrote this quickly, really putting little thought into it at all, whilst sat in the same chair I have for the past seven years. I wrote it as a quick end to my thoughts, I had to get them all out as much as I could. And you will all understand now, if this is being read out loud by the priest, that is Fr Mike,* (Here I imagine Fr Mike shall perhaps pause and nod) *that I asked him specifically to read it out, and that it was of importance, great importance, that it was read at the very end of the funeral, after all things* (Keeping the rhythm from earlier) *And so, I hope we are there, or here, even, after all things and at the end. So, allow me to begin proper from these lightly formatted quick notes of all my thoughts up to now at the end and after all things. Firstly, though I can't really say if it will be firstly, though I very much doubt I will go back and edit this, so it may very well still be first. It's not that I am dying, as many of you well know, it's just that this really is the last bit and I just need to get it out. So firstly, maybe, I am sorry.* (Fr will understand to intone this with a sadness) *Not to any of you I don't think, as I am not sure I knew any of you at all, or even knew myself, really. And of course, I can't exactly be sure as to who will have turned up, some of you I may have known but then I can't be sure of that. But in a way, I am very sorry, see, I am sorry for all the noise I made.* (Fr will understand that this is where the pace begins, so to speak, here, I imagine, the audience will have once more got comfortable in their seats, their pews) *You cannot imagine the extent of my remorse in the face of even my most minor squeak. Truly, if I am sorry for anything it's for the noise, all the noise, I was just so noisy,* ***all of you were none the better***, (Fr, I trust, will understand my emphasis) *and I am in the same boat. Now, I certainly wasn't the worst in this boat, but I made noise all the same. Let me think, see, if you converse, you sin. Yes,* ***if you converse, you sin***. (Fr will get the intonation, the intuited pause between this repeated statement *just right*, and some people in the audience, that might be just a handful, but even so, will really just get something out of that) *Look, I wrote this just before I fell all to pieces, and mostly I just want to say sorry even though I don't really know how to say sorry, and so I'm sorry, or I'm not, I don't know, and in a real sense I didn't fall to pieces it was just that no one came to see me, but I never wanted to see anyone or for anyone to come see me and would have preferred to have been left alone. Anyway, the point is that, the point is, the point is that* (Fr will intuit the importance of this, picking up the pace into a new rhythm) *everyone talks now and* ***no one says anything***. *Everyone just makes noise after noise, on top of noise, within noise, from noise, with noise. Everyone tries to fight the noise with more noise, and that in turn creates more noise.* (Here I imagine, or even feel, there may be a few laughs, though I trust Fr's stance and stature will retain the seriousness of this solemn and sincere moment) *Everything, all of this, all of that, it's all built on top of some notion that everyone should be heard and that everyone has something to say and that everything that everyone says is something that should be heard and should have been said at all. And many of you may, very rightly, would have wondered why I went to pieces in the way that I did, and it's because everyone talks and no one says anything. And that's why I became so sick, and so many of you gave all these other reasons why, but this* *is why, this is why!* (Here Fr, I imagine, will look up at the crowd, glaring at them for a second or two) *The noise makes you sick, and I would just wake up with this doubled-up headache and stomach ache every day, and I'd wake up and think of words like banging and throbbing and achy and belly and tummy, and then that would make me think of the word* ***yummy****, and then, in turn, I would think of* ***yum yum in my tum tum****. And so, every day, I would wake up and because of all the noise, of which I am not innocent in the creation of, I would wake up and within an instant have the saying yum yum in my tum tum rattling around my brain, merging with the headache and the stomach ache, it was truly sickening, I was sick, and it was because of everyone else. And this, in turn, all this tum tum yum yum business* (Fr must be careful here to not allow this talk to descend into silliness, I imagine, he won't, I trust him), *all this nausea brought about by noise, it made me think of a trainee lawyer who lived with me for a while. I lived with this guy,* (This is the only point where I feel Fr may naturally clarify that he is still speaking as me, and may repeat this but state *[my name] lived with this guy*, he will do this in such a way, I trust, that will be patient and planned) *a while ago I lived with this guy, this trainee lawyer, and I hadn't much room so he slept on an inflatable mattress in the lounge, and every day when I'd get up I'd hear this odd retching sound coming from the lounge, and one day, I got up earlier than usual and went through to make my coffee, and I found that he had his head over the bin, and it turns out that this friend of mine, now an acquaintance, this trainee lawyer who lived on my lounge floor, it turned out that he was so stressed and put out and fed up with life that upon waking, he would, every single day, without fail, as his first act of each and every day, projectile vomit into the bin.* (Fr will do well here, I imagine, to leave a generous pause) *And I remember I was quite stunned, but I remember also that quickly a large, spontaneous grin grew on my face because, well, in truth, and I believe and imagine and think we all agree, that such a way to* *wake up, is, in truth, and it is a real truth, utterly perfect. One wakes up and immediately negates life, immediately posits waste, immediately spews!* (Fr will do very well here to get this just right, as I imagine it) *It was beautiful, perhaps the most beautiful thing I've ever known. And that is how I feel about all this noise, that if only I could have been like my spontaneous friend, now an acquaintance, and upon waking, simply vomited up all the noise and started afresh. But no! I was going around with the reverberations of* ***tum tum yum yum, tummy yummy tummy yummy****, resounding and bounding and cascading around in my skull, a truly grotesque affair, awful, even. It really makes you feel very sick that* ***everyone talks and talks and no one says anything at all****. I'm waking up with a stomach ache and a headache, yum yum tum tum, like I said, every day just from the knowledge that everyone, including myself, is still talking, still just producing all this crap from their mouths, and these aren't even mouths that really talk, not really, and we all hear everything and say everything, and yet, no one hears anything because no one said anything, mouths open and all that comes out of each of them is just noise noise noise and I just couldn't have it anymore, I guess, maybe?* (Here, I imagine, the priest will begin to pick up the pace in the natural way, all the while remaining solemn and sincere at my demise) *Let's look at that or Let's take that apart or Let's analyse that or Have you ever thought about it like this? That's the kind of nonsense they state, dragging* ***us*** *into* ***it*** *as they do. And that's another thing, people can't* ***say*** *anything anymore, everything is an opinion, or a statement, or a proclamation, or a manifesto, or a saying, or a cliché, or a discussion, or a discourse, or a defence, or an attack, or some or other thing that has to be, and nothing is just* ***said*** *anymore, even though no one, of course, says anything at all anymore. And yes, they drag* ***us*** *into it all,* ***dragging*** *us into their noise as if it's worthy of anything at all!* (I imagine, here, that Fr means business, as they say) *And I question them, in my mind, in my mind I question them, I ask them, how about we don't do* *anything? And how about we don't say anything? And did that* ***need*** *to be said? And did you really* ***need*** *to say that? And do I need to be involved? And do I* ***really need*** *to be involved? In all this, do I really need to be involved in all this? How dare anyone feel it is their purpose, their calling,* ***their right,*** *to get anyone at all involved in anything at all that they do? How dare they!* ***How dare everyone!*** (Fr's volume here may encroach on the bounds of acceptability within a church, but he understands) *And that's the thing,* ***that is the thing,*** *everything has to be said now, everything apparently has to be said now, apparently everything has to be said now, if it can be said then apparently it must be.* ***If there is noise then it must be made!*** *How dare they! Lord forgive us all, right now! But he wouldn't, and even if he did, we wouldn't hear him because we'd be too busy discussing and conversing and dialoguing and maybe, even, perhaps, yes...chatting! There is no greater sin that chat. Chit chat chit chat chit chat, along with yum yum tum tum, these words* ***chit chat*** *rattle around, along with* ***yummy*** *and* ***tummy***, *inside my pained and* ***ever suffering*** *skull. Think about the most banal, vapid, empty, asinine, detrital, vacuous, and loathsomely boring idea imaginable and you can bet your silence on the fact that two absolute chit-chat chatterers are sat in a room half-chuckling about it, not even taking it seriously, smirking at what they say and laughing only through their noses in quick bursts, not real laughter, but habitual laughter, the grammar of a submissive imbecile. How awful! Grotesque, even. Shut up shut up shut up shut up!* (Perhaps, here, I imagine, Fr will get caught up and appear flustered, even) *I click anywhere or go anywhere or listen to anything and I think you didn't need to say that,* ***you didn't need to get involved***, *I didn't need to know this, I didn't need to hear this. But now I do, and it's your fault. No more! But there will be more...* ***there will always be more!*** *And sure, yes, quite, indeed, I imagine that we are all smiling and all happy on the outside and all accepting and all content but that doesn't mean anyone involved in these chats,* *these discussions,* ***is in any sense*** *happy about the whole thing. I mean, and I* ***do really and truly mean****, what are we all asking of these people, asking of each other, asking of ourselves, can it be anything less than our souls? I think not. And so when we converse, we understand that our souls, each and every one of our souls is on the line,* ***our souls are on the line each and every time we open our mouths****,* (Fr will, I imagine, look up at the parish with a glare that harks back to his own sermons on salvation) *and so, in the defence of our souls, for the defence of our souls, we do not speak at all, we cannot do it. There is no such thing as a simple conversation, there is only a meeting of souls who succumb to damage or manage to exit unscathed, this time,* ***this time they exit unscathed****, but what of the next, and the next, and the next, and the next,* ***the day will come when not a soul exists that hasn't been tarnished and ruined by noise****. Sure, yes, sure, lovely, here we are having a conversation about some or other intricate, beautiful idea or thought or memory, but we look to the left and find an advert for bolognese, look to the right and see a road crash complete with corpses of family and friends, look up and see some guy yelling that the end is nigh, we look down and find politics is at our feet.* ***What the hell have we done****.* (This, Fr will assert with a sternness, bolstering his own solemn and sincere approach to this talk) *The Fall of man, thrownness, an old lady trips and hits her head on a big old stump, it's all the same, it's all* ***gut wrenchingly tragic****. And yet it's all one and the same, for* ***all the people are one and the same****, and all their conversations are therefore one and the same, and therefores come rolling down and therefore one day you're just mucking around with your mates and the next you're just in the thick of it, you've become a schoolteacher, a lecturer, a politician, a person of influence, a VIP, a council member, hell abound...* ***you are on a committee!*** *You, sirs and madams, have become caught in the noise, engorging on all the parasitism that makes everything run. Lord please, I beg of you, forgive me!* (Fr may gesture with his arms here) *I guess, in the* *end, given enough time, not even that much,* ***everything turns into the one thing you didn't want it to become****. Give it a lifetime, a decade, a year, a month, a week, a day, an hour, even a sordid minute, and from one glance to the next that thing you sculped and nurtured and watched grow, from one look to the next, has become this monstrous spawn, and you wonder where it all went wrong, and you wonder then what it would mean for it to be right, and then you wonder then what it even was in the first place, at one point in time you have an idea in your mind, and the next there is this great fat pile of* ***putrid shit*** *on the floor in front of you, such is life.* (The words *putrid shit* will resound around the church quite unholy, but, I trust, and imagine, that Fr will understand, truly) *That's the reality though, right? That truly, and I mean it truly, I do, that it* ***is*** *life. Things can be going well and everything is right and you're doing what you thought you wanted and even earning* ***good money****, as they say, and yet when asked what's wrong, you can't put your finger on what it is, and people ask you what you want and you reply* ***Not this****. What do you want? Not this!* (Fr, perhaps, possibly, I imagine, on the verge of tears, the parish stunned) *You wake up one day and find you have everything only to look down and realize it is, and* ***always was****, in truth,* ***nothing at all****. What then? Any man or woman who can answer the question, the only question, of* ***What then? What next? What now?*** *now this is someone I would pay a fair chunk of change to talk to, though not all my money, as I like stability. Oh dear, what a state, what an absolute state. But we all, you see, ask people to display their hearts and minds and they...just do?* (Fr now, I imagine, openly distraught) *Is that any place for thought, out there, just...out there,* ***out in the open?*** *Is that any place for anything? I must repeat, I really must...it's not me,* ***it's you****. Wait, I mean, it's not you,* ***it's me****.* ***Half of our lives are spent making mistakes and the other half is spent regretting them****. I wish to be silent, and yet that silence is already invaded by the noise of the regret regarding the noise I've already made. Do you remember that time* *you-* ***Of course I do!*** *Of course! Cry havoc and hell, dear me, that noise, dear me I am ever so sorry for it all.* (Fr, here, will become sombre, perhaps even look over to the confessional, I imagine) *But then again, then again, we are, surrounded by the most vacuous pile of empty* ***shite*** *imaginable* (The word *shite* will, I imagine, exit Fr's mouth all caustic and horrid), *and the smell of it wafts all around—and you know, it's like, well, you know, well, it's like, kinda, I mean, you know, I mean, it's like, well, look, here's the thing, like, well, I mean, kinda, and you know it's like I mean kind of—* ***shut up!*** *In time anything you carve out that's different becomes a repetition, and* ***anything good becomes bad****, and anything new becomes old, and anything unique becomes the same, and* ***everything becomes anything****, and in time, yes, in time,* ***it's just all the same****, it's all just noise, filler. Yes! That's it!* (Fr raising his arms and now loudly proclaiming) *That's what people want! No one really wants to listen or watch or read or build or create or learn, people nowadays only want to have their* ***time filled****. If a single monotonous beep was entertaining enough, they'd just fill their time with it. People get up and fill their time, they go to work and fill their time, they come home and fill their time, and if they could, in their dreams they would fill their time. Death is the final filling!* (The priest must *not*, under any circumstances make this appear sexual) *Go fill yourself elsewhere! I'm sorry, I am, truly,* ***sorry, sorry, sorry****. But eventually, too many apologies beget the opposite effect. So, in truth—sorry and go away! Sorry and shut up! Sorry and get a grip!* ***Sorry and no more!*** *Take your pick. It doesn't matter anymore.* ***It never did****.* (And back to sombre, heartfelt, even, Fr will, I imagine, understand) *Everything can be read however the person filling their time with it wants it to be read, everything heard can be heard however the hearer wishes it to be heard, every conversation is an open book,* (This is clunky, but Fr, reading this multiple times beforehand, perhaps even rehearsing, will come in hard with the following) ***every signifier signifies all****, every word says* ***everything and anything****!* And it's all, all of it, taken in, drawn in vampirically, sucked in, hoovered in, vacuumed in, sucked up and in, and just ***abused*** (Will Fr spit here? my imagination allows him to, shocking!) *It's drawn in and used up, and none of it is put to any use, no one takes any of this in, no one fills themselves up and changes it any way at all.* ***Have you ever met anyone who ever changed in even the most minor way?*** (Glaring around at his parish, his mouth wet with saliva. I imagine) *On and on and on they talk, they don't stop. Every day. More and more. I see it. I see it. Every day there is just more stuff and therefore more stuff to talk about and people listen and...no one changes. I go there and I go here, and I go* ***back*** *there and I go* ***back*** *here, and I see her and I see him, and I go* ***back*** *and I see her and I go* ***back*** *see him, and maybe it's been 5, 10, 20, 30, 40, 50, maybe even* ***60 years*** *and they are just the same, they are the exact same, not a hair is different, and they've engorged on life, filled themselves to the point of bloating, and they're all filled up and they just, they just,* ***they just haven't changed at all***. (Anger, melancholy, eyes cast down and almost bellowing, weeping) *Everyone has severe indigestion, indigestion of the ego, indigestion of the self, indigestion from noise, and if it was all to digest, if all this noise was to finally be digested, there wouldn't be anything left, all the hot air would finally be let out like some rotten old dying dog's fart and there'd just be nothing left but some half-baked crap smell.* (Fr calms enough during this line that it lands solemnly, beautifully, even) *And yet people will* ***still*** *say have you heard of this or that it's really it good, it really* ***helped me****, I really* ***got*** *something from it, it's really good, it's really* ***great****, you* ***have*** *to, you* ***need*** *to, oh you* ***must***. ***Must what?*** *Must watch the thing that has led you to...be the* ***exact same*** *person you were 4 years ago? Why would I do that? Why would I do that* ***to myself?*** *How* ***dare*** *you!* (And Fr has brought it back up, into a furore, a fury, an outburst!) *Again, I'm sorry, really, truly, I am, truly, yes. But also, maybe not, I can't be sure. Look, if you want an apology consider it given, if not,* ***go away****, if not,* ***shut up****, if not,* ***please leave****, if not,*

*I'm not interested, I'm* ***not*** *interested,* ***I'm not*** *interested,* ***I'm not interested!*** (A final yell of *I'm not interested* from Fr, perhaps he will continue to yell this sentence over and over and over and over again, yes, yes!)

and here Fr's face, I imagine, is red and flushed and perhaps even covered a little with spit, and he is out of breath, and some people, though it may only be a handful, as I said, have left, and some are angry, and some are shocked, and if there is enough, others are tearful, others are sad, and others are changed. But here's the thing, and I just cannot help it, and I am stuck, and yet I have to get it down, as I imagine the people, possibly just a handful, beginning to leave, one by one, I imagine that Fr composes himself, gets himself together, and in doing so realizes he is still holding my speech, that is the paper upon which I wrote my speech which he originally took from his pocket. And I imagine, that, as some are standing up, and some are heading out, and some are chatting, and some have already left, I imagine, and I can't shake this, that as Fr goes to put the paper, the one with the speech written on it, back into his pocket, he accidentally drops it and the air gets to it and it lands a few feet away and, in my imagination, I am not sure if anyone else sees or not, and father is slowly bending down, and it's taking a while because he is old, and I can't see them, in my imagination I can't see them now, and I can't see if they see, if anyone saw, that Fr dropped the paper and half-scrambled to pick it up, and there it fades, and I go over it and over it, and every time, every time, the paper is dropped. Every single time the paper is dropped. Every time the speech is dropped, right at the end.

Printed in Poland
by Amazon Fulfillment
Poland Sp. z o.o., Wrocław

33369506R00141